Infinite Anatomies

SELECTED BOOKS BY RICHARD TRUHLAR

Terminal Intelligence (Mercury/Teksteditions 2011)
The Hollow and other fictions (The Mercury Press, 2005)
Dynamite in the Lung (The Mercury Press, 1999)
The Pitch (The Mercury Press, 1992)
Figures in Paper Time (The Mercury Press, 1989)
Utensile Paradise (Aya Press, 1987)
Parisian Novels (The Front Press, 1983)
A Porcelain Cup Placed There (Coach House Press, 1979)

Infinite Anatomies

STORIES BY
Richard Truhlar

TEKSTEDITIONS
Toronto, 2012

Editor: Beverley Daurio
Composition and page design: Beverley Daurio
Cover image: photo collage by Pearl Pirie
Author photo: Mara Zibens

Streets of This City Have No Names was previously published in *Rampike*, "Scientific Wonders" issue, 2011
Monologues for a Mannequin was previously published in *Permission to Speak: an anthology of new fiction* (Teksteditions, 2012)

First Edition

2012 2013 2014 2015 2016   5 4 3 2 1

Library and Archives Canada Cataloguing in Publication
Truhlar, Richard, 1950-
Infinite anatomies / Richard Truhlar
Issued also in electronic format.
ISBN 978-1-927367-11-7
Title.

PS8577.A75C67 2012   C818'.54   C2012-901936-4

ALSO AVAILABLE IN E-BOOK FORMAT

Teksteditions
www.teksteditions.com

Table of Contents

Introduction

A few years back, I experienced a 'sea change' in my writing. Up to that time, I had been exploring the phenomenon of consciousness, and the unconscious, in works of layered complexity and language — what could be considered 'avant-garde,' even though now I dismiss the term. This change was essentially a change in my self — in my perceptions, behaviour and attitude towards life — and it led me toward a different path for my writing.

From my childhood, the literary works that had inspired and thrilled me, and led me to be a writer, were those imaginative speculative fictions by the likes of H.G. Wells, Jules Verne, Edgar Rice Burroughs, and Edgar Allan Poe, and I've always unconsciously carried within me the desire to write such.

So this 'sea change' led me back to my early literary roots, and I decided to give myself permission to pursue the passion I have for speculative fiction. Hence this volume you hold in your hands.

In beginning to write these stories, I formulated an 'oblique strategy' as methodology to shape this volume. Firstly, I decided to write fourteen stories, since the letters of my first name and last name (each having seven letters) add up to that number. Secondly, for inspiration and focus, I decided to let the titles of musical and text-sound compositions be the leaping-off point for each story. During my mid-life, I had composed a significant catalogue of electroacoustic and electronic works with evocative titles, so I drew on them, allowing the composition's title to suggest the content or ideas for each story, yet not necessarily trying in any way to capture the feeling or atmosphere of the music or sound work.

So here then is my first volume of speculative fiction. I hope you'll enjoy it.   — *Richard Truhlar, 2012*

"So, Mr. Melmoth, you've written us a number of times regarding your complaints. What is it you're exactly upset about this time," said the wonderfully accommodating man seated behind the plastic desk. "And, be specific please, there are too many departments here handling grievances."

"A grievance?... Oh no, no, no, and not a complaint either... more an anomaly," said Charles Melmoth, seated across from this pleasant accommodating personage, "you know — it's one of those kind of unexpected social phenoms."

The accommodating man replied, "Anomaly... phenom... nothing my department can generally do for you; so what exactly is the problem?"

"My wife — she's disappeared," said Melmoth.

"That's not a grievance," said the wonderful man. "It's a statement, an imprecise statement, to be precise. So — have you been sexually abused by your wife? If so, you need to go to the Office of Sexually Aggrieved Males — office number 204 on your left when you leave here."

"No," said Charles, "I haven't been abused in any way... she's just vanished."

"Vanished, eh?" the bespectacled man mused as he took out a large tome from his desk and began turning pages. "Let's see... Vaguely Conflicted Person of the Criminal Type... no, that's not it... Validly Confused Person about Documents... no again... Vanishing Person of Unknown Origin... ah, that must be it. You need to go to Office 314."

"But she's not of 'Unknown Origin,' she's my wife and has lived in this city all her life," replied Melmoth.

"Well, we don't know that, do we? We don't know where she's from or where she's going. Please proceed to Office 314. The gentleman there hopefully can help you. The elevator is just to the right of my office down the corridor. Take it to the next level," and with that, the suddenly unaccommodating man slapped shut the tome and sat back with a smug smile on his face.

"Well, thanks for your time," said Melmoth as he proceeded to exit the Office of General Inquiries.

★

In the elevator, Melmoth thought about the occurrence that late afternoon of the preceding day. He had returned at his usual time from work. Coming through the front door, he had hollered his standard salutation, to which Vera had replied from the kitchen, "Just in time. Dinner's ready." He had hung his hat in the vestibule and entered the open space that served both as living and dining room. Vera, smiling triumphantly, had stepped from the kitchen, holding the silver platter upon which sat a succulent, browned pork roast with rosemary garnish — he could smell the rosemary… and, in the blink of an eye, she vanished into thin air, the platter and pork crashing to the floor.

Melmoth's jaw dropped open, and he crashed to the floor like the pork and platter, but in a faint, where he stayed until next morning.

Awakening, he began to mutter, "Vera, I had the strangest dream…" his arm reaching out to caress his bed-mate, before he realized he was lying on the floor staring at the living-room ceiling. Arising, a cold chill crept up his spine, as his eyes sought out his wife, only to encounter a pork roast, a pork roast and a platter only, on the floor, but no Vera.

★

Stepping from the elevator, Melmoth felt an ache he couldn't explain… *Oh come on, Charles!* he thought, *You know exactly why you're feeling this… she is a part of you, intricately woven into your nervous system, a distinct emotion apart from yourself, yet present in your thoughts, and as real as you are to yourself, and now she's gone!*

He opened the door to room 314, and was suddenly confronted with a stentorian voice declaiming, "Name?" Melmoth quickly moved to the only available chair, placed directly in front of this inquisitor who, behind his desk, seemed to be engaged in some obscure activity with his hands.

"Um… Charles Melmoth, sir."

"Date of birth?" asked the inquisitor of the Office of Vanishing Person of Unknown Origin.

"February 14th, 1950," replied Melmoth.

"I'm assuming you're here with a problem to solve… one which deals with a Vanishing Person of Unknown Origin. Am I right? For if I'm wrong, you needn't be here," said the inquisitor in a loud declamatory voice.

"It's my wife, Vera," said Melmoth softly so as to not to encourage any further stentorianism.

"Hmm… so your wife, this Vera, she is now, as we say, a Vanishing Person of Unknown Origin?"

"Well… " began Melmoth cautiously, "she's not unknown. I've known her for thirty years, and I know her background, her family, and her origins mostly."

"Mostly?... hmm, but Vanishing," and the inquisitor seemed to sink deeply into thought while his hands moved in arcane ways at some obscure activity.

"Ah, here it is!" the inquisitor shouted, now no longer inquisitor but a declaimer, "Right here… see?" and the bony forefinger of his right hand pointed down at the desk, as his face hovered, staring, a mere eight inches above his discovery. "It's the Tower," he said assuredly.

"What…?" asked Melmoth, his eyes trying to make out what seemed to be a card of some sort on the desk.

"The Tower, man… can't you see it? In the cards of the understanding of a Vanishing Person of Unknown Origin, the Tower represents prayer… your wife has gone to pray," explained the declaimer, smiling as if all questions had been answered.

Melmoth stared at the man, stared down at the card he pointed to, stared back at the man, and sputtered, "Wha'… Vera doesn't pray… she's a fucking atheist… she didn't go to any Tower to pray," and for the first time in his life Melmoth seriously thought about making someone vanish, making this declaimer of the Office of Vanishing Person of Unknown Origin vanish.

"Now, firstly, there's no need for profanities. I understand your acquaintance with the common vernacular," spoke the declaimer, "You either go or you don't go. Simple, really."

"Go where?" asked Melmoth.

"Well, to the Tower, of course," replied the declaimer in exasperation. "You must wend your way hence. Then you'll know why your wife goes to pray when she doesn't pray; but heed me well, there are many trials in the Tower, first and foremost being your encounter with The Gatekeeper who prevents the unwanted, the uncalled-for, from entering… then be prepared for any manner of being, all hostile, all your sworn enemy," and the declaimer then picked up the card of the Tower and gave it to Melmoth. "You'll need this," the declaimer said. "It's your token of access."

"But I have no enemies," Melmoth replied.

"No matter," replied the declaimer, "you must now journey to the Tower. There is a small lighthouse out on the islands off this city's coast. There you must go to find your wife."

Melmoth stared at the declaimer, then at the card of the Tower in his hand, and reluctantly left.

★

It was a pleasant afternoon when Melmoth disembarked from the ferry to the Point, the westernmost of the city Islands. The sky was clear blue but for the occasional cloud scudding by. He had a forty-minute walk before he would arrive at The Lake Light, the small historic landmark that was the first and only lighthouse of the city's harbour.

It's only eighty-two feet high! — that's no Tower, he thought to himself as he viewed the abundant flora surrounding him along the roadway he traveled towards his destination. Melmoth loved plants — so much so, that early in his youth he had become an amateur paleontologist, searching certain areas in the south-western part of the province, where erosion had uncovered the past, uncovered the trace-forms of prehistoric plant life. In the present, he enjoyed being the chief tender of the Cool House in the The Gardens, the botanical conservatory in the heart of the city.

While inexplicable negative emotions and irrational thoughts had besieged him throughout his existence — he had fought them off, knowing somehow that his transport through this short life must, of necessity, concur with creative thought and deed… and, of course, there was Vera, a gentle, compassionate woman, who also struggled to evolve beyond negative self-evaluation, and he knew that he would forever be her partner, her lover and her friend. He had met her in the Cool House.

"What is that? It's lovely," she had asked as he was about his watering duties.

"It's a Kashmirian Cypress," he had replied as he looked into two of the loveliest amber eyes he had ever seen.

While meditating upon his disappeared loved one, he happened to look up and find himself but a number of yards from The Lake Light — this so-called Tower of a Vanishing Person of Unknown Origin.

You've got to be kidding, Melmoth laughed to himself, while appraising the diminutive structure.

Within seconds, a figure appeared from behind the lighthouse — a man, his clothing and wide-brimmed leather hat all in black, and who seemed at ease, and in no hurry to speak, as he slowly sauntered towards Melmoth.

"You're The Gatekeeper?" Melmoth queried, while thinking to himself that he had fallen into an elaborate ruse.

"You are?" asked the man.

"Charles Melmoth."

"And you are here for?"

"My wife, Vera," replied Melmoth, fumbling in his pocket and producing the card of the Tower of a Vanishing Person of Unknown Origin.

"Are you sure it's she who's vanished, and not yourself?" asked The Gatekeeper, taking the card from Melmoth's hand.

"Wha'… what?" Melmoth sputtered.

"Well… you're here aren't you," replied the man in black, all the while displaying nothing more than a distant demeanour, "and you shouldn't be. Besides, there is no answer here for your question since there is no question for your answer."

Melmoth just stared at the man.

"If you enter that Tower," said The Gatekeeper, pointing to the structure behind him, "if you enter through its door, you will encounter…" and the man paused but showed no emotion, "Well, you're free to do so, of course, since I have your card… and it's not my role to either encourage or dissuade any wandering soul like yourself."

"I want my Vera back," said Melmoth, his voice slightly cracking.

"It's your choice," said The Gatekeeper, and slowly stepped aside, as Melmoth moved towards the Tower door, opened it, and without hesitation stepped through.

★

"Charles? Charles, are you awake?" queried a voice from far away.

"Vera?" Melmoth seemed to croak, as he began to sense motion around him and opened his eyes, somewhat uncomprehendingly since he could not remember closing them.

"It's okay, darling. I'm here. You're doing okay. Just rest. I'm here with you."

"Vera?" and Melmoth's eyes began to focus, the face of his wife looking down at him smiling, but with a trace of recent tears on her cheeks.

"You've had a minor heart attack, darling, but the medics say you're okay. We're in the ambulance now on the way to the hospital," Vera said.

"How... ?" began Melmoth.

"Shhh... don't try to talk. You had just walked in from work, and suddenly collapsed in front of me. You're going to be okay. I called Emergency immediately. They say it's very minor."

"Vera?"

"Yes, darling," said his wife.

"Vera, do you pray... ?"

STREETS OF THIS CITY HAVE NO NAMES

So it was that, one summer day, during his break between first and second year at Clare College, as Clarence Regan wandered about the neighbourhood in Cambridge, that he found a lovely park that abutted the Cam River embankment. The park was well manicured, the grass having been appropriately cut; but under a small tree, he spotted a lone flower growing from the lawn, somehow having survived the mowing by the Parks maintenance workers. He ambled over and sat before this flower, the type of which he could not place to this day. Seating himself a small distance from the flower, he cleared his mind of any thought whatsoever while focusing his perception upon the plant. Not an easy task for a twenty-one-year-old, but he persisted in forcing any thought or voice from his mind, and within some time began to fully relax, even though he was concentrating with all his will upon it. His mind cleared. He felt an immense peacefulness and solidarity within himself. He was all eyes and empty mind. Before him was this strange creature or entity for which he had no name, because he would not allow the word *flower* to enter his mind, and he saw that it moved slowly, that it shifted itself according to the position of the sun — and that it was constructed of many particles of light that flickered and moved incessantly throughout its body. He sat there in this intense focus for perhaps a full hour as if in a trance of awe.

This was not a religious experience, as he was to find out later; and was not brought on by imbibing any drug whatsoever, since his days of experimenting with such were well behind him. So, at the time, he simply regarded it as an exercise to relieve his mind of the strain of study — science and mathematics being his intellectual pursuits at the College. Truth was, some strange occurrence had happened to him, unbeknownst to himself, which would alter the world around him, and not just for himself.

★

"But think of it, Joyce — what if this notion of the End of Times, this apocalyptic yearning that is central to all religions... what if it's not in a time to come, but has already happened, is happening, and will continue to happen?"

Joyce Draper looked across the table at her friend. "Rubbish," she said in a tone devoid of emotion. "Empirical reality exists whether you perceive it or not. The old koan-like *If a tree falls in the forest...* is a question that points more to our arrogance as subjective beings than to the existence, or non-existence, of an objective world."

Draper rapped her knuckles on the wooden table-top, "That's there, whether I'm here or not, and it'll be here long after I'm dead if it doesn't end up in some landfill. As for you..." and Draper paused to look into her friend's eyes. "Look, Clarence, we're all mortal. You're not unique in this. Some of us comfort ourselves with fables, fictions, religions in order to assuage this painful awareness of..."

"This isn't the same," interrupted Regan, "I'm not delusional. I just *know* that, for instance, this table will cease to exist when I die."

"Clarence, I'm a scientist, a paleontologist. I look at fossils all day — they're the trace-forms of previous existences. They tell me that creatures walked this earth long before I came to consciousness. They're evidence of a time continuum in evolutionary life... have you seen a psychiatrist?" Draper suddenly asked, breaking her line of thought.

Regan sighed. "I'm not delusional," he repeated, "and you've known me most of my life. You know that I'm a scientist, as well."

"Yes, but, from what I understand, you blokes are wrestling with proverbial angels in your Quantum theories... what, with alternative universes, the seen and the unseen, and all that. I'm not surprised by your thinking, Clarence. I'm more concerned that you'll mistake your abstractions for empirical evidence... look, sorry, but I've got to go — duty calls. Perhaps we can pick this up tomorrow — same time, same place?"

As Regan watched his friend exit the coffee shop, a cold feeling of dread swept over him.

★

Joyce Draper was a tall woman, but unimposing, graced with the aura of a gentle demeanour. She was never seen to be openly angry, perhaps only slightly irritable at times, and would look everyone in the eyes with curiosity rather than apprehension or prejudice. Her field, marine-life paleontology, had honed her perceptions and given her an almost obsessive attention to detail. Her extreme rationality, however, was not born of abstract thinking, but rather of a sensuality arising from intense observation of the surrounding world.

The next day, as she boarded the bus and found a seat, she was thinking of Regan who she would meet in twenty minutes at The Cosmic Coffeehouse. His ideas, of course, were controversial, and she had often played devil's advocate in order to spur him into expressing his most considered theories. She cared for him; one might even say she deeply loved him, but not in any romantic way — this man, who was considered one of the top Quantum theorists in the world, and was being compared to Darwin in the iconoclastic effect his thoughts were generating amongst his colleagues, was simply her best friend.

Odd, she reflected while gazing out the bus window. *Perhaps it's stress. It's not like Clarence to doubt reality, no matter how weird reality can get. It's almost ludicrous for such a scientific mind to consider all reality existing just for itself. I'm not going to cease to exist just because he does,* and she then stopped her train of thought. *Perhaps he really does need therapy.*

Walking into The Cosmic Coffeehouse, she took a quick scan across the room, then asked the regular barista on duty, "Hey Joe, seen Clarence yet?"

"Not yet, Miss Draper," said the young man, momentarily glancing up from foaming a latte.

She was about to walk towards their regular seating place, when she stopped suddenly.

"Joe, where's our regular table?"

"Don't know, Miss Draper; wasn't here when I opened this morning," Joe replied while continuing to work on a customer's order. "Maybe the boss moved it last night; maybe he needed it for something."

Somewhat perplexed at having to choose another seat, she ordered her coffee, and found a table by the large front plate-glass window from which she could watch for the arrival of Regan. For some reason, she felt agitated.

Sensing Draper's mood, Joe called out, "If you're gonna be here for a while, you can ask Mr. Waites, the boss, about the table. He's comin' in this afternoon to work on the books. I know you like that spot in the back."

★

An hour passed, and deep lines had begun to appear on Draper's brow. She felt a bit confused and concerned. *It isn't like Clarence to simply not show up,* she thought to herself. *He's meticulous about keeping appointments.* And though she had forgotten her cell phone at work, she knew Clarence might suspect such and phone the coffee house if he were going to be delayed.

She was about to get up and leave, thinking she'd phone Clarence from work, when she heard a loud voice.

"Joe! Where in hell's the table back here! Where'd you move it to?"

"Nowhere, Mr. Waites. I thought you took it," came Joe's reply.

Draper looked up to see an exasperated middle-aged man whose eyes were darting this way and that around the coffee shop.

"Tables just don't walk away!" yelped Waites. "Were both doors locked last night, and did you notice if they were this morning?"

"Yes, Mr. Waites. Anyway, who's gonna break in and just steal a table?"

Waites shook his head and disappeared into a back room.

Draper stood with her mouth agape, a variety of discordant thoughts cascading through her mind, yet one distinctly insisting itself — *This does not compute!*

★

When Draper arrived at her office at The Paleontological Association, her first act was to phone Clarence's home number. She stood beside her desk with a quizzical look as the voice in the receiver told her that the number she had dialed was not in service. Thinking she had misdialed, she rang again, but received the same prerecorded message. *This is ridiculous*, she thought as she keyed in his cell-phone number, only to be told that such a number did not exist.

For a minute Draper stood frozen, her mind full of conflicting thoughts, then phoned his lab number at the Institute for Advanced Physics. A voice answered. It was Brian Henley, Clarence's colleague and research partner, whom she had met a number of times at receptions.

"Brian, is Clarence there? It's Joyce Draper."

"Hello, Joyce," replied Henley. "No, he hasn't come in yet. I thought he was meeting with you for coffee."

"He was, but he didn't show up. I've phoned both his home and cell, but…" Joyce was suddenly overcome with fear, "both numbers are not in service."

"Odd," was all Henley could reply, then "Maybe there's a problem at the phone company?"

"I thought that at first, but his home and cell numbers are serviced by different providers," said Draper, while feeling she had to calm herself, think rationally.

"Well, I'm sure he'll show up, and when he comes in, I'll get him to phone you right away. Are you at the office?"

"Yes, but I won't be here," she replied, "I'm going over to his apartment. There might be something wrong. Brian…" and Draper hesitated, "are you blokes working on something… well, you know… dangerous, maybe top-secret stuff that could lead to… ?"

"Nothing of the sort," said Henley with some surprise in his voice, "just particle tracing — Sherlock Holmes on the trail of the muon — that sort of thing."

"Okay, then. It's probably nothing, but I'll take my cell phone. Call me if you hear from him.

"Joyce — do you want me to meet you there?" asked Henley. "It's a slow day here and, anyway, without Clarence I can't move forward with the work."

"Sure. I'll be at his apartment in half-an-hour," and Draper hung up.

★

When Draper disembarked from the bus, she saw a large horde of people gathered down the block. There were police cars and fire trucks and ambulances. She began to run because that's where Regan's apartment building was located. She didn't see any smoke, but... Suddenly someone grabbed her left arm.

"Joyce!" and she looked up to find Henley's face, his very pale face, and his very large eyes, eyes full of questions, "It's gone..."

Draper looked down the street at the crowd, then back at Henley, a shiver coursing up her spine.

"The apartment building, his building... it's gone," said Henley in a dazed manner, "It didn't burn down, didn't fall down, didn't blow up, it's... just gone."

Draper, feeling slightly panicked, began moving toward the crowd, dragging Henley with her. *The table*, she suddenly thought, *it's gone too!* And she remembered Regan's words, "this table will cease to exist when I die."

When she reached the crowd, her eyes sought out the building... but it wasn't there. As if it had never been built, in its place a perfectly vertical rectangular empty space was visible, the borders of which were the perfectly smooth walls of the row-house-style attached apartment buildings on either side; the ground but a dirt lot with various and sparse weeds growing, some of which had blooming flowers signaling their habitation there over time.

"Brian?" was all Draper could say, as she felt his grip on her left arm loosen and fade away, and turning her head to look at Henley at her side, found no one there. "Brian!" she nearly screamed as her eyes took in a slight shimmer in the air where Henley had been, a slight shimmer in which she could barely discern a pair of astonished and pleading eyes that then blinked out of existence. Then she looked at her left arm, which he had gripped, an arm that seemed to be becoming more transparent by the moment.

★

"Ma'am, can you hear me?"

She slowly came to consciousness, feeling herself lying prone on the ground, her eyes barely making out human forms about her.

"Here — take a sip of water," and her head was raised gently. "You gotta nasty bump on the back of your head, but nothin' serious," she heard as she took a drink from what she assumed was a bottle.

Two persons were kneeling at her sides. She slowly sat up, her mind unusually empty and remembering nothing of the incident.

"What happened? Where am I?" she asked.

"Well, ya were knocked down, miss, trying to cross the road. But the carriage just grazed ya slightly, so no real damage. Stupid driver said you appeared out of nowhere. Some people need their eyes checked. Here, let me help ya up. Do ya feel ya can stand?"

"Yes, thank you," she replied and got to her feet. She found herself standing on a cobbled road, the boardwalks on each side full of strangers gawking at her. She wiped down her billowy dress, feeling somewhat embarrassed by the situation.

"Can I assist you in any way, ma'am?" asked the young man.

"Yes, please. I'm feeling a wee bit odd. I just need directions to my father's shop. I'm on my way to my first day's work, you see. He might be angry that I'm late. Do you know it — it's Clarence's Cosmic Confections. I've forgotten the actual shop number, but it has a large sign out front painted with spinning stars."

"I know it well, miss. The chocolates are my favourites. If it pleases, I'll accompany you," he replied.

So taking his arm, Joyce proceeded to walk with the young man towards her father's shop, looking forward to her first real work in the world.

"What's your name," Joyce asked, because for some reason she felt comfortable and at ease with this young man.

"Brian, ma'am, Brian Henley. Presently at Oxford, ma'am, where I'm studying these new theories of Mr. Darwin's," and Brian looked into the young girl's eyes and smiled.

It was five o'clock in the evening and the sun, having yet not gone down in the west, was still throwing rays that illuminated the tips of clouds below. Herbert looked down upon them while he swizzled the drink on the tray before him. He took a short sip of his cocktail as he gazed in wonderment at this display of nature from his unnatural perch at thirty-five-thousand feet above land. *Lips of fire*, he thought to himself, the alcohol leading his thoughts to lyrical imaginings and, taking the notebook from his travel bag, mused that perhaps this was the start of a new poem. He never feared flying. The odds were against such aerodynamic death — *better odds in being run down by some drunken teenager*, he thought, so he settled back, pen in hand, ready to inscribe...

"This is your captain. The weather is fair. We're on time, and should be landing in St. John's at seventeen-hundred hours and ten minutes. The crew of CF-104 wishes to thank you for flying with Air Canada."

Herbert ignored the intercom, and proceeded to write his poem, as another and very different image forced its way into his head:

> The inoccupation of bodies
> aboard a plane at 35,000 feet is
> a spider silence

He sat back, taking another sip of his cocktail, and thought about how much he hated planes... *It's like being in an oversize cylindrical tin can — the air's terrible, and I'm packed in with these people, these shallow ghosts with their gadgets that beep and whine... they talk into them constantly as if...* he was thinking as the captain's voice suddenly blurted through the intercom, "We seem to be heading into a heavy bank of fog. Nothing unnatural for St. John's, but it may delay our landing by ten minutes. If you have a connecting flight, we have radioed ahead, and they are aware of our delay. We'll keep you posted."

Herbert looked at the three lines he had written. *If any of them even thought of writing something like this… well, they can't…* and he looked about at his fellow passengers, as the slow haze of alcohol began to break down his inhibitory conscience — a conscience he had relied upon throughout his life to ensure his survival both as a physical and mental being. He sank back in his chair, not allowing himself further thought, for he knew instinctively it would be unproductive, and gazed out the window, seeing nothing but a darkening slate grey.

★

Herbert had dozed off for a time when he was abruptly awakened. He was being jostled to and fro in his seat. As his eyes came into focus, he saw luggage flying out of the overhead compartments all down the aisle. At first he thought, *it's only turbulence*, before the entire plane began to fall, his body being nearly lifted out of his seat and, but for his seatbelt which he always had fastened snugly, his head hitting the overhead call station and pod-lights without injury. His ears picked out a hubbub of voices shouting for the stewards, someone swearing "What the hell!" and small children's shrill voices reaching hysteria, as the engine noise increased incrementally, the sound signifying an inevitable, unstoppable descent.

The intercom suddenly blared into life as the captain nearly shouted in a restrained voice, "All passengers, secure yourselves for crash landing," and as quickly fell silent.

Herbert felt something swiftly whisk by him from behind, and his eyes then caught the body of one of the stewardesses flying head-over-heel down the aisle and crashing into the door of the cockpit, her body crumpling to the floor. The shrieking, crying and engine noise continued to increase until he heard it — the sharp loud crack — and his eyes beheld, a mere fifteen metres in front of him, the rending of the cabin wall, as if someone outside was using a can-opener around the circumference of the plane's metal hull. Just as Herbert saw the two parts of the plane separate, he was thrown back violently into his seat, and the plane was crashing.

★

Herbert didn't know how long he had been unconscious, but before he opened his eyes, his olfactory sense already had been busily collecting a number of smells that reminded him of burning plastic and upholstery, of things organic also burning, and perhaps also mouldering. His hand went to his face where it encountered a viscous wetness. *I must be bleeding…* he thought, and finally opened his eyes. A natural disorientation, of course, would be common to a man having just traveled through a traumatic disaster — but Herbert's cloudy perceptions were forthwith skewed and reinforced by what he saw. Beyond him there rose a number of seat rows that ended at a large opening that was above him. In fact, as Herbert began to understand, and feeling himself to be practically lying on his back, he was looking upward at a forty-five-degree angle, and the opening was the end of the split aircraft through which he noticed, emerging sporadically from a drifting fog, gigantic trees that, oddly enough, resembled cyclamen with dense foliage of dark green leaves splotched with silver.

He began moving slowly and languorously, his body being pressed back by the gravity of his position, his limbs aching, and his eyes still in a somewhat disoriented state. He was still buckled in his seat, and fumbled for a while until the belt was undone. Feeling that there was no major damage to his body

— his limbs felt unbroken, his back sturdy and, beside a bleeding forehead, felt no severe gashes in his flesh — he proceeded to pull himself upward seat by seat towards the open end of the plane. Conscious of various forms hulked in the seats on both aisle sides, he refused his eyes to direct themselves away from the opening above that would grant exit from the carnage. Reaching the torn and jagged lip of the plane, which was hung with cables and other hardware, Herbert looked back into the shadows of the craft's interior. He, of course, knew what would greet his eyes — the bodies of passengers, of men, women and children, some missing limbs, some heads, and some having been unbuckled and tossed about until all that remained was a flayed torso. Nausea rose to his throat, and he looked away. He peered over the torn edge of the plane, and estimated about twenty metres to the ground, a ground that intermittently peeked out of the fog swirling all about, and seemed to comprise small bushes and reeds. He had luckily been wearing his leather jacket, which he had donned when it had been announced that they were two hours away from St. John's, and which he now used to cover the sharp edges of the hull. Gathering his strength, he hoisted himself over, hung momentarily, and then dropped, having the prescience to keep a grasp on his jacket. Herbert found his fall broken by the ground itself, which was swampy and oozed through with water, the muddy morass feeling like a firm cushion when his body dropped upon it. He rose, still holding his jacket, which was now sodden, and looked about. The fog was still thick but, with a constant attention to his surroundings, he could discern a great gash in the swampy ground, which showed the direction the other half of the severed craft had traveled in its crash. Hoping that someone still survived, he set out slowly, sloshing along the side of the gash in the viscous ground, and, momentarily glancing back, saw that the fog had thoroughly obscured any sight of the wreckage from which he had escaped.

★

Trudging along through the swampy morass, Herbert noticed that the fog was thinning and dissipating. How far he had traveled he had no idea. He stopped and looked up. These strange towering trees seemed to raise themselves hundreds of metres into the sky, a sky he could only see as speckles in the dark massive canopy above. Here, an eternal twilight seemed to be the common illumination of the day, and he could not imagine what night would herald. Other forms began gradually to be discernible as the fog lifted. He noticed large metal fragments that reminded him of wings, then while stumbling a moment, his eyes surveyed a dotted landscape of luggage and carcasses. Looking at his feet, he saw that he had tripped over a human arm half-submerged in the muck, and then looking forward he saw the remnants of the plane's forward hull, a mass of twisted, gnarled metal.

Making his way through the debris, he eventually reached the cockpit, which had been spilt open, and looking in saw the corpse of the captain smashed flat against what remained of the forward controls. *But where's the co-pilot?* Herbert thought to himself, suddenly starting to look about the craft, since there was no trace of a second body in the compartment. Nowhere forward of the smashed front of the plane could he see a body, thinking that the co-pilot perhaps had been ejected through the cockpit window.

Herbert now felt exhaustion coming upon him, so he found a relatively dry piece of luggage to sit upon and ponder what to do next. *Must've overshot the mark, crashed into some swampy area around St. John's*, he mused, his utter fatigue disallowing any anxiety... *or, we fell short, so if I keep in the direction the plane is pointing, I should reach the city's outskirts at some point*, and having concluded thusly, he arose reluctantly and began plodding forward, hoping he'd get out of this wet mess and attain solid ground shortly.

★

Having struggled for what seemed an hour or so, pushing his way through tall reeds and plants, he saw ahead that the land sloped upward in a gradual ascent, and knew he was coming to the end of this fetid marsh. Once attained, he sat for a while on the gradient of what he assumed was the beginning of upland country. His mind was strangely empty of thought, with only brief images of the past catastrophe flickering occasionally in his inner eye.

He looked at his jacket that was splotched with muck, grabbed some newly fallen leaves nearby to scrape it off, and put it on, feeling now chilled by the constant dampness of the swamp. He slowly stood and walked up the incline, thinking all the time that perhaps he had veered off course. With all the thrashing through reeds taller than he, and stumbling, falling over rotten logs, he suspected he may not have had proceeded in the direction he had first determined. But these thoughts quickly vanished as he crested the rise of the slope. The trees had gradually thinned and disappeared as he had made his ascent, and now Herbert beheld an open plain before him.

The plain had small streams and rivulets running through it, and was covered with various flora — mostly horsetails and ferns, with differing species of cyads and conifers clustered in groups and dotting the landscape. It was then Herbert realized that he was nowhere near the city of St. John's, and perhaps not even in Newfoundland — for the plain stretched far and away, ending in the distant horizon where the indistinct forms of a large mountain range reached into the sky. For a moment, with something akin to despair overtaking him, he looked back. The solid wall of strange gigantic cyclamen towered before him, but now he could see its canopy — a solid cap of leaves with masses of bright green ivies entangled and reaching upward, swaying in the wind.

Herbert collapsed upon the rise into a sitting position, and once again looked upon the plain. His thoughts swam discordantly, his eyes darting this way and that as they noticed some new strange detail in the scene before him. In the moment, what had begun as an unformulated and slight feeling of despair congealed and overwhelmed him, and he began to sob uncontrollably. *Where in hell am I? What am I to do? Where am I to go?* he variously cried inside himself. He sat for a long time in a state of inertia, allowing all the pent-up emotions, from the crash to the present, to air themselves, to relieve his self of their burden because somewhere inside he knew he would need all his wits and reason in the time to come. His head drooped to his chest, and he focused on his breathing in order to calm himself. Looking at the ground in front of him, his eyes began to puzzle the odd markings in the dirt, and within moments he understood.

"They're footprints!" he exclaimed aloud. Three sets of prints went down the gentle slope to the plain, and he could see, by the shoe marks, that it was a man and two women. He felt calmer now as he set out towards the flatlands before him, his eyes following the path made by this trio whom he surmised were the other remaining survivors of the crash.

★

He had been walking for some time, moving through a sparse area of stunted cyads and conifers, his eyes ever upon the human trail, and only momentarily looking up to see the environment about him, when he caught sight of an odd formation rising from the ground off to his left. Finding a large, leafless, fallen branch from one of the cyads, he thrust it into the ground vertically to mark his position, and set off towards the structure, wading through a dense sea of waist-high horse-tails. About five metres away from his destination, he came out upon a sandy expanse that seemed to circumscribe a large mound — for that is how it impressed him. It towered at least twenty metres, was perhaps forty metres across, and was constructed of sand that looked as if it had been cemented. The walls of this architecture were smooth, and occurring irregularly along the base were circular orifices about three metres in diameter. *It's surely been constructed, but by what?* Herbert thought.

As he moved closer, with the intention to inspect the openings in the wall, his ears were alerted by a loud rustling in the compact thicket of horsetails off to his right. He froze on the spot, not daring to move in case he drew attention to himself, and hoped it was merely a squirrel or hare or some other small fauna.

As the creature broke through the wall of horsetails on to the sandy enclosure, Herbert's eyes could not quite apprehend what they saw. It seemed like a gigantic string of dark red fused beads from which, extending on both horizontal sides, were bent twigs pumping in a furious motion upon the ground. Within moments, however, the map in Herbert's memory threw up its analogue. His heart began to race, his head turning quickly to scout over the horsetails for his planted branch, his eyes finally finding their goal, and he ran, thrashing through the undergrowth towards his marker and perhaps his only affordable weapon. As his eyes sought out the horizon for some safe haven, he spotted a copse of very tall cyads and, now running in desperation, he reached his previous path and scooped up the branch. He held it as a club, as he dashed for the copse, hearing, close behind, the rushing, rustling creature.

Reaching the group of cyads, he chose a tall one that was leaning slightly and clambered up its rough, scaly bark. Feeling he had attained sufficient height, he shifted himself into a position facing down along the tree trunk, the better to club the thing on its head if it attempted to climb towards him — and on it came, the scuttling millipede, a good three metres in length. Its antennae twitched to and fro, the mandibles busily opening and closing, while the flat eyes of its face stared straight at him. Reaching the bottom of the trunk, it hesitated.

"Get the fuck outta here!" screamed Herbert, panic rising within him.

The creature hissed, attempted its first ascent, and hesitated again. Herbert, with violence, smashed his club against the bark in front of him. The millipede hissed again, and began backing off. It remained at the tree's base for some moments, antennae twitching, hissing softly now and, turning its body, began to move in the direction of the mound. Relieved, Herbert began to understand — it had only been protecting its nest. But now, with the full events of the day trying upon him, and noticing that it was twilight, he sought out a resting place, and found a space amongst the cyads above ground where the large tree branches were thickly intertwined and matted with leaves. He was able to lie there, albeit uncomfortably at first, until he fell into a deep and dreamless sleep.

★

Herbert awoke as the dawn broke. His body ached from its cramped position in the tree limbs. His stomach growled, and his mouth was parched. He lifted himself gingerly, and in a cautious manner climbed down from the cyads, all the while keeping an eye on the surrounding terrain. He saw no evidence of the millipede about. Finding his original trail with little difficulty, since he surmised it was somewhere between his position by the trees and the mound, he again was soon following the footprints, which shortly came to a clear stream of about ten metres across. He knelt down by its side in some soft grass, drew fresh water to his mouth with his cupped hands, and drank thirstily. Looking into the stream's depth, he could see no fish, but his eyes caught a slow motion across the underwater rocks. Curiously he reached down, felt something roundish that was slightly larger than his hand, and pulled it from the water. It was, it appeared, a giant snail.

But can I eat it raw? Herbert asked himself, while remembering how much he had enjoyed escargots, though always baked or sautéed. Searching the pockets of his jacket, he found his favourite writing pen, and carefully, slowly he was able to pry the slug from its shell. Its body was the size of a large sausage. The creature began squirming the moment it was in the open air. Herbert took it and placed the slug on a large flat rock nearby. Then placing the rock directly in sunlight, he waited until all the creature's motions had ceased and he knew it was dead. Using the pen as a spit, he poked it through the middle of the body. Forcing any thought of what he was eating from his mind, Herbert bit off a good chunk and began to chew. *Well, it isn't cordon bleu,* he thought, *but it's somewhat tasty, if a little tough.*

Having finished his meal and drunk from the stream once again, he found the footprints, and saw that they proceeded off along the water's edge heading upstream. Herbert looked up at the sky, judged it was now probably mid-morning, and began following the trail left by the survivors.

★

The plain wasn't really a plain at all, not in the traditional sense of rolling vast savannah or the Great Plains of North America. Rather, it was an expanse comprising numerous differing environmental features and micro-climates. This accounted for the frequent changes Herbert saw as he traversed the landscape. He noticed, for instance, that the lush area of cyads, conifers

and horsetails from which he had come was gradually trans-
forming on his left into a slightly marshy area (though the
ground he walked upon at present was suitably solid) and
which was characterized by great swaths of ferns, through
which ran tiny rivulets. The stream and footprints that he was
following ran along the edge of this area, and paradoxically to
the right of him extended a sandy expanse of rolling dunes,
the monotony of which was broken by what he recognized as
mounds, having the same characteristics as the one he had encountered before.

Herbert stopped as he saw that, just a short distance in
front, the stream bent to the left and began cutting through the
fern field. He looked over the wide, dense expanse of waving
fronds, watching for any movement in the distance signalling
the position of the survivors and, at the same time, had an odd
thought: *Why am I alone? Why didn't the co-pilot, assuming that
one of these three survivors is the co-pilot... why didn't he come back
to the tail-half of the plane to search for other surviving passengers?
He surely would have found me.*

Asudden, his sight caught a brief flash, as if, somewhere out
there in the sea of fronds, a mirror had reflected the sunlight.
His vision focused on the remote spot from which it had come,
his eyes straining and intent, and gradually he could discern a
faint motion, giving the impression of small coloured flags signalling in semaphore. The flash came again, and he could finally
make out three bodies moving hastily and erratically through
the field of ferns. Herbert, with no hesitation, dashed forward,
following the path of the stream, for he felt that its course
would lead him towards the moving figures. As he ran, he
began to hear sounds coming from their direction — shouts
and screams. He was able to keep his vision on them since the
surrounding ferns were only waist high, but somehow the picture in his eyes was unclear — there seemed to be a darkling
cloud moving about the three figures.

As Herbert gained on their position, he slowed his pace, beginning to realize there was something very wrong here — this wasn't a cloud — it was a horde of flying creatures, all flashing bottle blues, greens and reds as the sunlight glanced off their bodies. Their wingspan was a good metre and their bodies two-thirds of that — they were dragonflies, and they were swarming the three people who ran hither and thither in panic. Herbert traversed the remaining distance within minutes and, without thought for his own safety, charged into the scene brandishing his tree branch, which he swung ruthlessly, smashing the insect bodies into the earth or into pieces or into the sky after which they plummeted to the ground. After perhaps five minutes, he stopped swinging and, panting heavily, saw that the remnants of the horde had fled away in various directions over the field of ferns.

★

"Well, if it ain't a fucking hero," Herbert heard from behind him and, turning, perceived the source of this comment.

The face his eyes met was swarthy. Its head had a severely triangular shape tapering from scalp to chin. The nose was long and slightly hooked. The mouth was thin and tight, and the man's eyes were small and coal black. His hair was scraggly and he was of thin proportions, more wiry and agile than delicate. He wore a bright blue sweatshirt, denim jeans and brown loafers. He looked at Herbert with an expression of cynical amusement.

"You're not the co-pilot," said Herbert, more as a statement of fact rather than query.

"Nope," said the man.

"But the co-pilot must be alive. His body wasn't in the cockpit or anywhere around the wreckage."

"Nope again, buddy... saw the body, sure... but then it was dragged away by some giant fucking thing lookin' like a cross between a frog and a 'gator," replied the man.

Herbert saw that the two women, who had fled the drag-onflies, now approached and stood on either side of the man. One was tall and slim with long blonde hair and hazel eyes. She wore a red silk blouse with cream-coloured pants that flared at the ankle and was shod in high heels. The other was of a normal build for a woman slightly above two-and-a-half metres in height. Her hair was short and wavy and deep auburn in colour, and she wore a cotton iridescent green shirt, black denim jeans, and track shoes.

"I'm Tracey," said the blonde.

"And I'm Evelyn," said the other.

"Name's Pedro," said the man, "and what's your name, hero?"

Herbert glanced at all three in succession, feeling a distinct dislike towards this Pedro, and replied, "Herbert... Herbert Wells."

"Well, Herb," said Pedro, which made Herbert wince inside since he detested nicknames, "Where d'ya think we are? It don't look like any Newfoundland I know."

Herbert looked over the swaying fields of fronds, remem-bering all that he had encountered thus far, and his poetic imagination began to suggest a variety of improbable 'what ifs.' What if, for instance, they had been blown off course by a vi-olently strong hurricane that took the plane in hand and flung it down the seaboard coast, the plane ending up crashed on some remote, uncharted island in the southern Atlantic? And perhaps this island, even more severely than the Galapagos, had been cut off from the natural march of evolution, had become frozen in a prior prehistoric age, but what age he could not think. The only ones he remembered were the Devonian, the Ordovician, and the Jurassic, mainly because of an amateur in-terest in fossil collecting and films he had seen. Yet dimly in the back of his mind, he seemed to remember something about an

Age of Insects, but couldn't remember its proper name, nor where it came in the evolutionary continuum.

"I don't know," Herbert said, and looked at the three other survivors. Then he looked again out over the plains, "I don't know," he reiterated, "but I don't think we should stay here."

"And where's there to go?" Pedro sneered.

"To those mountains," Herbert replied, ignoring the thin man's attitude, and nodding in the direction of the distant range, which now seemed somewhat closer than from his previous positions, "I think we'll be safer if we reach higher ground. Perhaps we can find a cave…"

"Ya, with some fucking huge monster in it!" Pedro spat the words at him.

"I think he's probably right, Pedro," said Evelyn.

"What the fuck do you know?" and Pedro turned on her with vehemence, "He knows about as much as I do, and that's nothin'."

"Well," said Herbert, "that's where I'm going. Hopefully we can reach the mountains before sunset. Anyone else want to join me?"

Evelyn walked to his side. Reluctantly, the other two followed when Herbert and Evelyn had strode a short distance. Tracey, who had said nothing except to introduce herself, declaimed "Shit!" as she, with a little difficulty, began negotiating the uneven ground in her high heel shoes.

★

Whatever place this was, it had obtained the characteristic of an intense humidity, as if there was an abnormal abundance of oxygen just waiting to be set afire. The sun seemed to beat upon the plains without respite, and no cloud in the sky had been visible throughout the day. Yet occasionally a thin mist would arise and float above the ground, since the plain was rife with numerous small streams and creeks. There were no birds to be seen, and the only flying creatures the quartet of survivors chanced upon in their entire trek were the large dragonflies that seemed to make their home in the fields of fern. As the day drew on, the quartet continued to wend their way upstream, following the small waterway they had initially encountered. Soon it became obvious that the stream was widening, and then they saw, a short distance ahead, that it emptied into what was a large river. Looking across the river, Herbert could see the foothills of the mountains rising just a short ways from the opposite bank.

"We're almost there," he said as he reached the edge of the river and, eyeing it, estimated its breadth to be no more than a quarter kilometre.

"I ain't crossin' that," spoke Pedro defiantly, who had come up from behind and joined the other three, "I saw that friggin' frogocroc or whatever, and I betcha it lives around water, like that swamp we come from."

Herbert turned to him quickly and hissed, "Then stay here."

The two women remained silent as Herbert made an inventory of the surroundings. They had left the fern fields behind just a short while ago, and now found themselves in a sandy, rocky area. Large cyads dotted this landscape, and seemed more abundant along the river's edge. Spotting a very thick fallen tree trunk of about five metres in length, Herbert said, "We'll use that. Find some branches you can use as paddles," and he proceeded to drag what he considered 'nature's canoe' to the river's edge.

It floats just fine, Herbert thought, once he had wrestled it into the water, and turned to the others with a slight smile, while saying, "Come on, get on."

For a moment, the others stood, good size branches in their hands, reluctant to follow, while Herbert mounted the front of the trunk.

"I ain't crossin' that," Pedro echoed his previous statement, but this time uncertainty crept into his voice. He really didn't want to be left behind, but had to complain — *Who made this guy leader, anyway?* he thought.

Herbert ignored him. The women clambered aboard the trunk, with Pedro finally giving in and following, a look of resentment on his face. They sailed out, and shortly had reached the other side, which was a sandy beach along which ran two high rock outcrops.

Debarking, they quickly set foot upon the beach, and stood surveying the sand and rocky formations before them. As Pedro was about to make some snide remark, or perhaps assert his own opinion of what they should do next, an increasing audible noise, like shuffling and scuttling combined, caught the entire group's attention. From between the outcrops there dashed two black chitinous bodies, each about a metre in length. Their eight legs each carried them at a swift pace, five times faster than the millipede Herbert had encountered before and outran.

"Fuck!" cried Pedro, but before he could move, one of the creatures was upon him, had raised its tail and stung him.

Herbert shouted, "Here!" attempting to draw the creature's notice, as he made a dash obliquely from Pedro, while Tracey was frozen to the spot and screaming, as the second of what now were apparently giant scorpions quickly advanced upon her.

Evelyn had run to one of the rock outcrops, scrambled up to a ledge at a safe height above the sand, and was now finding rock debris that she tried to pelt the creatures with, but they moved too fast, and her efforts were in vain. Herbert ran and reached Tracey just as the creature reached her and heaving his branch brought it down upon the creature's back, but not before the scorpion had jerked its tail forward and stung the woman. There was a large cracking sound as the anthropod's carapace came apart, the creature writhing and carouseling in pain until it had inadvertently thrown itself over upon its back where it remained twitching.

Herbert glanced over to Pedro who was crumbling to the ground, and saw the second scorpion scuttling speedily towards himself. It was a unique moment in Herbert's life as his reason and intuitive instinct synchronized to do battle with this creature. The scorpion, reaching him, thrust its tail stinger forward as its front left and right pincers snapped at his ankles. Herbert reflexively hopped back, avoiding the attack, while the scorpion paused momentarily to regroup for the next attack. Again it lunged forward and again Herbert hopped back, the man being untouched, but now fully aware of the creature's pattern. When next the creature thrust at him and he hopped back, Herbert saw that momentary pause, jumped to a place on the left of the scorpion and, with all his might, swung his still-faithful tree branch at the creature's stinger. He connected like a batter at the plate for a home run — the scorpion's stinger coming apart and splattering all over the sand. There issued a high pitch screeching from the creature and it fled in haste. Herbert watched it recede over the rolling sand, and disappear far off in some conglomerate of rock formations.

Herbert's first thought was of Tracey and he wheeled about to see her already collapsed on the sand on her back, her spine arched, her limbs in violent spasm until her body sank into a deathly stillness, foam beginning to gurgle from her mouth. His eyes sought out Pedro. His body lay still, foam bubbles issuing from his lips and his skin becoming a darkish shade of blue. Herbert stood stunned, until a soft sobbing encroached upon his consciousness. He looked to the sound's source and his eyes found the figure of Evelyn where she lay unhurt and safe upon the outcrop ledge.

As he reached the rocks and began to climb towards her, his thoughts took an unpredictable turn. All his instincts, all his intuition, combined with his reason and knowledge of the past, conspired together to tell him that there was no civilization here, no humanity apart from himself and this woman, this woman he had met through an accident in time and space, this woman that he now knew would be his mate, their species depending for its survival upon their conjugal joining. For, if he was correct in his deepest and knowledgeable suspicions, they were the only humans in this particular world, wherever and whenever this world had its existence.

Now seated beside her on the outcrop ledge, he watched as she sat up beside him and wiped the tears from her eyes. He saw she was shivering, took his jacket off, and wrapped it around her shoulders. She looked at him, at first timidly then, seeming to see the unusual glow in his eyes, she smiled.

Seeing her smile, he smiled too, and in a complex of uncertainty, irony and whimsy said, "Evelyn, I have the feeling we're not in Kansas any more," and as the twilight gathered about them, they drew closer together for warmth's sake, and perhaps they drew together also for something not yet understood.

Imagine, if you will, that you are seated in an aircraft traveling over terrain unknown to you, and for a moment you glance down. Your eyes catch a detail far below the clouds, and it feels as if you have remembered another time, another place, where your dreams had become reality. You swizzle the drink on the tray before you, thinking of whence you have come. Where shall you go now, O voyager?

It's time to celebrate, my new little friend. Tonight we celebrate! Pay no attention to those shifts of colour in the sky. You've seen magenta before, as well as burnt umber, so cease your mewling. We created that spectral tapestry. It's the ceiling we painted in order to stop the blasphemous sunlight from entering our eyes. Here — take this flask... yes, I know it's only cheap corn liquor, but it's the best I could acquire, given the recent failure of other crops.

You are young... too young to know anything, so let me instruct you, and relate to you how that sky came to be. What? You say your skin is flaking? Well then, you should always remain in the shadows as I do. "And if I don't?" you ask... well, more corn liquor for me... Hahaha.

You ask too many questions. What do you mean, "Why are we celebrating?" It's the Thousandyear Eve, of course, the first of its kind — the eve of the first millennium of our victory over the unbelievers. "What's an unbeliever?" you ask... ah, you try my patience. What have your parents been teaching you? Ah yes — my apology — they both died recently — I remember now. Probably like you, they didn't keep to the shadows. I can't believe the ignorance that surrounds me! You see that sky up there? It seems solid, doesn't it? But it's not. That's an illusion. Those various fused bands of colour that seem so solid? We call that 'atmosphere.'

What's your name? Hijira? Well, shut up now! No more questions, just listen...

★

I was young once, like yourself, but my parents taught me to keep in the shadows. I know my old man's skin now looks like leather, tough and scored, but in my youth I had no problem with this flaking you're complaining about. In fact, looking at you, I would guess you've been eating from the land, from what they're growing from the soil. That's why the veins stand out on your skin so, and your skin is that pale azure colour. I always ate what was grown in the Vaults, even though it had little flavour... but I'm still alive, and my skin hasn't turned blue.

I see you're being polite now, and are asking if you can ask a question.

"What Vaults?"

Ah, I see you're from another caste. Well, there are those of us who were given the responsibility for the continuation of our species. You would be unaware of this, given your place in our society. Your kind generally have grown up in the ignorance you've preserved and, for some warped reason, you supplanted in the stead of your natural intelligence.

Look... your parents are dead. You have been following me for days now, like some lost animal. I'll make you a deal, little girl. I'll save you from an early death, and reverse the damage being done to you — give you beautiful soft, amber skin instead of that blue, flaking hide you inhabit — and, in return, you will be at my bidding. You will speak only when spoken to, although, given your ignorance, I will allow you to ask questions if I see it is fitting.

You agree then? You do have beautiful eyes, you know. I love that subtle green glint in them...

★

So, to answer your question, the Vaults were built a millennium ago. Their primary purpose was to shelter our people against destruction by the unbelievers. Since we were victorious, we were able to leave the Vaults after a century. The land, however, had been devastated. Those of us with the knowledge we maintained from reading the great Books knew that the land would poison us if we grew crops from it and ate the harvest. So we converted the Vaults, found underground natural springs, whose water had not been contaminated, and began a program of hydroponics. You don't know that word, I see. Well, it just means that we grew our crops in water basins instead of soil.

The Books? Well, we never show them to those of your caste, but since you're now my property, you shall have a glimpse of them. Here... I'll just slide them out of this casket I keep them in... Why, yes, they are made of metal!... very thin sheets... and you see all those raised dots on the metal? Those are words, language... all you need to do, if you know how to read, is run your fingers over those dots and knowledge becomes yours. It would take some time to teach you how to read, but if you're good to me, perhaps I will.

It's getting late, and we've talked enough for now. The darkening outside has begun. We should retire and get some rest. Over there is a closet... yes, that's it. Blankets are inside... get them and make the bed over there in the corner. I'll join you shortly.

★

Aaah... Hijira, what a dream I had last night. The colour bands in the sky had dissolved, and in their place was a delicate soft blue palette. I was standing just outside this habitat, my bare feet resting in warm sand, and looking up. The darkening came suddenly and the sky turned blackish, but the firmament was punctured with pinholes, and light from beyond seeped through, so I knew then that He who helped us vanquish the unbelievers was still our Watchman. The air was fresh and, in the distance, I could see that nearby sea, long evaporated and now salt flats, newly sparkling in the night's light. You stood beside me, silent and compliant to my will — your delicate eyes drinking in the same vista, your body softly glowing in a new skin — and I called out, "Oh little one, I am yours, your master and slave."

Why are you interrupting me? You hurt? You didn't enjoy last night? Well, it will pass, you'll become used to it. After all, it was what you were built for, and you'll see the benefit once what grows in you sees the light of day. I can't believe your parents didn't tell you about this.

No matter. I have a surprise for you, my adorable one — breakfast! Some of my hydroponic engineer friends over at Vault 22 have worked, over a number of years, to bring a dream to fruition. They grew trees — can you believe it! So, this morning, we reap the benefits of their intellectual labour, and breakfast on *fresh figs*. Have a bite!

What do you mean you can hardly taste anything? Perhaps it's your body — perhaps your tongue and olfactory equipment aren't working. Well then, I think it's time to start your treatments, and revert the damage that's accrued to you. Here, take this soft chair, and sit back. Relax. Yes, I know it's an old hypodermic needle, but it still works fine. So, don't fret. I'll give you the first injection, and you'll see — your skin will start to return to a natural colour in a few days. I think five injections should do it.

★

You've gotten very big. Yes, I see, you're like a ripe melon there, aren't you. What, cramps? That's normal, just like when we were in the bed that first time — all good things require pain and suffering, but the rewards...

Now listen... people in the caste have begun to talk. You've been wandering around the compound, talking freely, and your mouth is getting us in trouble. You're carrying a new recruit within you, a new member of our species — they like it —

but keep your mouth shut. The last thing I want right now is to have to exterminate you. I hope you understand.

That said, and if you'll obey me, I want to confide in you. I know this goes against the dictum of my caste… but, I now feel differently about you. You have proven your worth to me, and… I think I care about you… I don't have a word for how I feel…

What? You don't think such a word exists? What are you saying? I taught you to read. I'm sure you can find the appropriate word. I sure hope so… and the sooner, the better, since you're due soon. You know what's going to happen, don't you? We've discussed it. I'll do the delivery myself. It'll go smoothly. I want my special moment to do this. The rest of the caste won't know about it, even though they're expecting it. Then I'll present him to them — and it better be a boy.

★

Hijira — what's going on? Where is the little monster? We have to stop him. Just out of the womb and he's already out in the compound. I heard screams. A friend told me that Kayla's hut was attacked — her uterus was torn out of her and splattered across the walls of her shack while her breasts had been gnawed off!

Why are you looking at me that way? Why has your skin turned green?

Diego Ramirez had found the perfect site for his new resort, a private haven that would accommodate family, friends and business acquaintances equally, and would as well provide all visitors with an experience not found with other resorts that were scattered throughout the Spanish countryside.

He had grown up in Barcelona, and followed a relatively normal education until he reached university. It was then he discovered architecture and pursued an intensive course of study. Not satisfied with simply being a dreamer, a planner, a blue-print designer, Diego took part-time work in the construction trade, where he dirtied his hands learning of every conceivable type of material that could be used to create buildings, while at the same time continuing his studies at school.

Both unfortunate — his parents had died when he still a boy — and fortunate — they had left him an estate of considerable wealth, Diego had felt driven most of his life, driven to fulfill some nebulous, unformulated dream, a dream of creating an environment of thorough beauty and security, where one could feel at ease at all times. It was not utopia he wanted — such could never be a reality given the vicissitudes of nature — yet at the same time he felt a primitive need to control his environment, a creative need to be able to build his surroundings, formulating them according to his wants and comfort.

So, having finished his university degree, and with money left to him in trust from his parents' estate, Diego established the Dreamscape Construction Company, which, over the years, became one of Spain's most recognized and prosperous architectural firms, and more than that — a company that actually built what it dreamt. Such was Diego's motivation that he had to be directly involved in the materials and erection of each new edifice.

So it came to be, after some time, having been successful in his career as well as his personal life — he had married in his late twenties an imaginative and compassionate woman, Adora, who had borne him a beautiful daughter, Ofelia — that Diego decided to retire, even though he retained supervisory control of the Company, and pursue his unformulated dream at the ripe age of forty.

★

Diego traveled far and wide over the Spanish countryside, finally coming to a stop at the Tabernas Desert.

"Here it is, the place I've been looking for, the place where I can build," he said.

His friend Alberto looked out over the vast terrain of arid arroyos, hoodoos and mountains looming in the distance. "Diego, this is *malpais*, no water except for some morning frost or dew, rains only in the winter and scarcely at that. Besides," continued Alberto, "this is protected as a wilderness area. The authorities won't let you build here."

Diego, also looking out over the terrain and not at his friend replied, "Yes, I know, not right here, but about two hundred yards back," gesturing with his arm to the country behind him, "is where the Preserve officially ends. I'll build right on the edge. I've already bought the land. Ahh, Alberto, it's so clean, the desert is so clean. I cannot think of a better place — the air hot and dry but pure — no pollution here, Alberto — and so far away from civilization. Yes, it is as you say — protected."

He turned and walked back to his jeep, Alberto following.

On the way to the city, Diego began talking. "When we get back to Almeria, I'll phone and have the Company come down from Barcelona. It's all set, you'll see, ground-breaking ceremony within a week — the materials, you should see the materials Alberto..." now glancing at his friend, finally acknowledging his presence, "the finest alabaster, cedar and marble you've ever seen!" His excitement rising, as within himself rose an image, the realization of that once-nebulous dream soon to become reality, he continued, "and with the expert crew I've assembled, we'll have it done in no time."

They were silent for a while, then Alberto began, "You know, I met that writer friend of yours."

"Who — Ramiro?" the other replied.

"Yes, and we got talking. You know how he's always doing research for a book — a new novel or whatever. Well, it seems his publisher asked him if he could do a novel with this area as its setting, thought it might be popular with the tourists."

Diego glanced at his friend with an air of disbelief.

"And you know, the funny thing is, Ramiro accepted," Alberto seemed to conclude.

Diego replied, "So... he does have to pay the bills."

"Yes, but he told me something strange. He said that, in pursuing his research of the Tabernas, he came upon reports of many individuals having disappeared in the area, and of one report in particular. Apparently, a man came out of the desert raving about how all of his comrades had been killed by creatures, but before he could give more of an account, he suffered severe convulsions and died of stroke."

Thoughtfully but skeptically, "Alberto, with the exception of jackdaws and other small birds, a few species of small reptiles and perhaps hedgehogs, there are no *creatures* in the Tabernas."

And with that they ceased talking.

★

The building went more slowly than Diego expected, mostly due, however, to his meticulousness as well as obstinacy concerning the overall utility that the place would serve. So, for instance, he had a large deep basement carved out of the bedrock upon which the hacienda would sit, and which when finished would provide both a root cellar and a very large underground entertainment den to which he and others could escape those days of scorching, intolerable heat to play billiards or watch films while sipping cold cocktails.

The hacienda was one storey, but elevated and enormous, spreading off in all directions like a many-limbed creature splayed on the desert floor, its walls made of the finest lily-white marble with inset smoked- or stained-glass windows in a large variety of shapes and sizes. There were multiple bedrooms, washrooms, kitchens, dining rooms, along with strategically placed saunas near large indoor swimming pools constructed to appear like hidden lagoons with waterfalls emptying into them, as well as obligatory intimate general- purpose rooms that could be transformed into performance spaces for soirées of music and poetry. The ceilings were high and cathedral-like, being simply the insides of the gabled roof tops, with skylights placed strategically to illuminate the paintings and sculpture that graced all rooms.

Outside, the array of numerous terraces and sub-terraces leading down to ground level were all connected surrounding the hacienda, so that here, one found a small shaded patio for quiet reading, and a few yards on and up would come upon a sunny cedar deck accommodating barbeque parties. Everywhere along the terraces were myriads of plants — yuccas, agaves, palms, flowering hibiscus, as well as ferns and reeds where artificial ponds had been built.

Perhaps the most audacious and incongruous part of the estate, however, was the wall. It stood seventy feet away from the extremities of the hacienda, was twenty feet in height, its top being convex, was two feet thick, and made of solid obsidian. It provided beauty in discord, contrasting sharply with the brilliant white of the hacienda and the light grey of the desert soil, for it was thoroughly black.

★

It took more than a year. Finally having the entire place lavishly furnished, the pantries and bars fully stocked, and every amenity provided for, he felt ready for its inauguration. He would bring his family down, of course, but also invite Alberto, as well as Ramiro and his lover María; and while he had initially thought of the hacienda as a resort, a retreat, a place of sojourn, perhaps he could show them that there was no necessity to live back there, live in those smelly, ugly cities of civilization, but rather they could reside here as a colony of family and friends, enjoying each other's company, and the beautiful environment he had created in this wasteland.

So they came — family and friends. At first, a type of awe showed in their faces, as they realized the extent to which the dream had manifested itself, how one man's vision could reclaim the wastes, mold it into a virtual paradise, as if mankind itself had reclaimed Eden. As they settled into the day-to-day, the awe was slowly replaced with feelings of pleasure and comfort, but the sense of living in a special place apart from the rest of the world never left them, and even though they knew they would return to their cities to work or take care of business, Diego had convinced them that this was *their* refuge, one to which they could return and live in as long and as much as they wished.

★

One day, during an afternoon barbeque on one of the upper deck terraces, Alberto approached Diego, who was leaning on a railing looking out over the desert.

After standing beside Diego for a while, slowly sipping a marguerita, he said, "So it seems what I said over a year ago had an effect upon you."

"What do mean?" asked Diego.

"Well look, look at that godawful wall. It's like a fortification to keep some army out. Truly, Diego, you don't mean to tell me that my mentioning a few men going missing in the desert was the reason for that wall? And just because some lunatic, who'd been out too long probably looking for dinosaur bones, then suffered sun-stroke and began seeing things that weren't there — well, I mean, you didn't take that seriously, did you? You yourself told me that there's nothing out there but birds, snakes and some other small harmless mammals. So I looked it up, and you were correct, just as you told me. It's right there in the encyclopedia."

Diego continued to gaze over the desert. "I don't know. Perhaps in some subliminal way it affected me that I didn't realize... I mean, I started to feel protective of all this," and he waved his hand around in the direction of the hacienda, "started to feel the need to ensure the safety of what I was creating, to feel afraid that if I built this without any protection whatsoever, something would come here and destroy everything, including us."

"What something?" It was Ramiro, who had been quietly listening a short distance away.

"I don't know," Diego replied, "but perhaps you can tell me... I mean, you've done research on this whole area, and Alberto told me what you had told him. Is there any more? Have you found out any more about those disappearances?"

Ramiro approached the other two men, and in a gesture of camaraderie, put his hands on their shoulders, as he moved up against them and whispered, "I don't think this is the time for this — the women, you know, you don't want to frighten them. Let's meet after the barbeque."

Diego moved away from the men. As he came up to her, his wife Adora looked up at him with a wry smile. "So, what are you boys dreaming up now?" her voice was deep with affection.

"Adora, what do I do now?"

"What do you mean?" she replied.

Diego looked at his hands. "I've built all this... I mean, it's finished... it's been my dream, something to aspire to, and it's finished. What do I do with the rest of my life?"

Adora took his arm in hers. "Oh, you'll think of something. You're always having ideas. That's what I like about you — you're always on the move, creating, building, thinking."

"But I need a challenge," Diego said looking into Adora's eyes, feeling a great amount of love for her.

"It will come Diego, just be patient. Now, why don't you mix me one of those wonderful margueritas of yours."

★

Alberto made a bank shot and sank the three ball.

"There's not much more, really," said Ramiro.

The three men had been playing billiards in the sub-level den for about ten minutes, at first none of them speaking.

"There are routine disappearances in the desert... you know, like the guy who decides to commit suicide and walks into the sea... some just walk into the desert, and their friends and loved ones never know what happened to them." Ramiro paused, taking a sip of Amontillado sherry. He continued, "But this one event, that I had mentioned to Alberto, was different. There were more details that made me suspicious. Firstly, the man who came out of the desert was a noted archeologist, not some crazy, and he was known to have put together a crew to explore the southwestern Tabernas." Ramiro took another sip of his sherry.

The other two men were silent, unmoving and listening.

"The second detail, of course, is what that man said. I told Alberto that he had raved about his crew being killed by creatures, which I suppose implies some thing or some things that could overpower a man, like a wild wolf perhaps. I'm sorry, Alberto, I was being vague when we spoke that time. What that man actually said was that his comrades had been bitten to death." Ramiro stopped speaking and looked at the other two men.

Before any of the men could utter a word, Ofelia burst into the den. "Papa, Papa, come see, come see."

Diego, as if coming out of a trance, looked at his daughter. "See what, my love?"

"The cloud, Papa, the beautiful cloud," she was visibly excited.

"But, Ofelia, you've seen lots of clouds."

"Yes, Papa, but this one's different. You can see it from the upper terrace."

"What's different about it?" Diego asked, now becoming interested.

"It's near the ground, Papa, over the desert, so low, I've never seen a cloud so low before. It seems to flow along the ground. Oh Papa, it's so pretty," and as she finished, the men looked at each other.

"Let's go see," said Ramiro, and scooped Ofelia up into his arms, all the men quickly moving towards the upper deck terrace.

Upon reaching the terrace, the men moved to the railing and looked out over the desert.

"See, Papa, see the cloud," Ofelia said excitedly, Ramiro still holding her in his arms, and they all saw it, the cloud, the lily-white cloud, moving across the floor of the desert, perhaps thirty feet above the ground, at times seeming to pour down into an arroyo and flow out again. It was about three miles distant from the hacienda.

The air around them had been still, but slowly a breeze began to build, which a few minutes later turned into a strong gale. The gale was blowing in off the desert, coming at them from the direction of the cloud.

No one spoke, their eyes all intent upon the approaching cloud. "I've never seen a cloud like that before," Ramiro spoke.

"It's so compact, so defined... and there're no other clouds around, the sky is clear." It was Alberto speaking.

The gale had grown even stronger now, making their eyes water. Yet they continued to watch as the cloud continued towards them.

When the cloud was, perhaps, a mile out, Ramiro hissed, "That's no cloud... I don't know what it is, but it's no cloud," and they all saw it now, saw that what, at first, seemed to be one mass, one moving mass of white, was actually a throng, a throng made up of thousands of white spheres the size of large beach balls, and in fact, some of them would bounce, bounce upon the desert floor, bounce until they had gained enough altitude to simply be carried by the wind, while others simply wove up and down in the gale's current.

"Shit," whispered Alberto.

Diego turned. "In the house everyone," he said, and they quickly moved towards the hacienda doors.

Inside, Diego instructed, "We'll meet in the west common room, the one with the floor to ceiling windows. We'll be able to see it coming from there. I'll get the women."

The two men with Ofelia moved off as Diego dashed towards the kitchen.

"Adora, María," Diego called as he burst through the kitchen door, "get food and water and juice quickly."

The two women were briefly startled, then saw the tension and concern in Diego's face.

"Wha'..." began Adora.

"No time to explain, hurry," as he began collecting smoked sausages, bread, cheese and other foodstuffs.

"Ofelia..." Adora nearly cried.

"She's fine, with Ramiro and Alberto. Hurry, we'll meet them in the west wing," said Diego, and with that the women sprang into action gathering what they thought they would need.

★

When they had all gathered in the west-wing common room, Diego explained the situation to the women and continued, "I hope we'll be safe here, whatever it is. The house was solidly built, the window glass thick and shatter-proof, and we have food and drink to wait it out," and for the first time since they had been on the terrace watching the cloud, his whole body sagged and he collapsed into a soft chair.

Ramiro and Alberto were standing in front of the large plate-glass windows, looking down upon the desert plane.

"The wall won't make a difference," Alberto motioned to the twenty-foot high obsidian. "They'll just fly over it."

Ramiro said nothing.

"I give it two minutes before they're here. The wind is stronger now."

When it came, Diego stood up, gasping. The women and child sat huddled together on a sofa, staring with saucer eyes at the windows, while Ramiro and Alberto remained rooted to the spot where they had been. And then they all heard it: a thudding, as if numerous large, soft objects were colliding with sections of the hacienda.

Suddenly María shrieked, as two or three of the white spheres bounced off the plate-glass windows simultaneously, Ramiro and Alberto staggering backwards momentarily. Then, it was if the thudding turned into a roar, and they watched with horror as the spheres began to accumulate outside the windows, piling on top of one another, creating a wall of spheres, each sphere four or five feet in diameter, lily-white and appearing silky.

"But..." Alberto began, not knowing what really to say, turning to Ramiro beside him, seeing the other man frozen to the spot with a dreadful look upon his face, then turning to look at the space where Ramiro was staring.

For a moment, nothing, then he saw it, couldn't help but see it, tearing itself out of the silky sphere, its body the size of a man's hand, eight legs, the black bead-like eyes set upon its face, its whole chitinous body the colour of blood, and the fangs, the two poisonous fangs. Thousands of them now began tearing themselves free from their spheres, spheres that had been woven by them, woven out of web, spheres that would be light as silk, that would act as their transports upon the wind.

The thudding having stopped, now other noises arose, that of scuttling, millions of legs scuttling, the sound cascading across the gabled roof tops, across the outside terrace floors, up alabaster columns, and the sounds of scratching or clawing as the creatures searched for crevices, apertures, any way to get into the hacienda, to get to their food, constituting the six humans they could see through the plate glass windows.

A high whining began, more like a faint screeching, made up of thousands of tiny voices, which became frenetic, growing louder and louder, grating upon the ear, a sense of frustration and hostility in the sound as it transformed into a screaming, the howling of voices in unison, issuing a battle cry.

★

For a full hour, having been frozen with astonishment and fear, the six humans had not moved nor issued a sound since it had begun. A thorough silence descended upon the hacienda. All eyes had been focused upon the large plate-glass windows, the other side of which only showed the piled web spheres, hanging in tatters, empty, with no sign of their occupants.

Diego began moving to the hacienda vestibule, the others remaining where they were, still under the spell of dread.

Upon opening the hacienda doors, Diego was confronted with a mass of tattered, thick web that filled their entire frames. Tearing at it with his hands, he broke through the sticky mesh of silk, and stepped out on to the front porch deck, itself covered completely in web — and something else as well. The gale had subsided. There was only a slight breeze. Diego crouched down, his eyes showing curiosity, his hand reaching out, and he picked up one of the small red bodies. This one was perfectly intact, yet showed a large gash on the underside of its abdomen, out of which a type of green plasma substance oozed. Most of the others had parts of them bitten or torn off. They were dead.

Ramiro came up behind him, stood looking at the scene.

"When they couldn't get to us, they turned on themselves," Diego mused, slowly standing, his eyes gazing out upon the desert. "I think the university will be interested in this," he said finally, as he handed Ramiro the little red chitinous body, and proceeded into the house to be with his wife and child, feeling for the first time in his life a doubt — a sense he still found hard to acknowledge — that he was still not safe, not secure, from the Other.

THE MIRROR IS ALWAYS EMPTY

Every day, every day! Harkness cursed to himself. *It's ridiculous... every day, cutting my self shaving...* as he opened the door and entered the boardroom on the sixtieth floor of Globin Global Incorporated.

He took his place quickly, finding the nearest empty chair and, looking up, noticed that others, like his self, had tiny pieces of tissue clinging to their chins and upper lips. This did not reassure him in the slightest, even though it had been his decision to join the corporation, given the benefits that would accrue to him in terms of wealth and employment longevity. He turned his gaze to the head of the table where James Keats sat.

"Well, gentlemen, the good news is that our stocks are up, the company is thriving like never before, and you'll all receive a hefty Seasonal bonus," said Keats, "and I would like to congratulate you all on such wonderful work. Most of you have been with us for some time," the President smiled, "and those of you who are new to GGI, while I'm sure your transitions into our company may have been difficult... well, you've all performed in exemplary fashion. So, as a personal sign of my gratitude, I want to invite you all to my home for a soirée this Christmas Eve. I'll have my secretary email you the directions to my place, and I look forward to seeing you all there. Please feel free to bring your spouses."

The meeting broke up, the President and company veterans exiting the boardroom, leaving Harkness and the two other recent recruits staring at one another.

"Jonathan — you got a *spouse?*" asked Renferd, the youngest of the trio, and stressing the last word with sarcasm.

"Girlfriend," replied Harkness.

"I got a spouse," said Helsen, the third man, "likes nothin' better than to suck me dry… can't wait to get her hands on my monthly paycheque."

Harkness sighed. Then, trying to divert the conversation, asked, "Hey, do you think we should take something to this soirée?"

"Nah, from what I've heard, Keats puts on quite a spread each year at this time. It's like he's trying to remind himself that he's human," Helsen chuckled.

The three men fell silent, and proceeded to leave the boardroom for the elevator.

★

Being winter and five p.m., the sun was already setting when Harkness stepped out from his company's tower on to Bay Street, in the commercial heart of downtown Toronto. He looked up at the grey, overcast sky, and saw the beginnings of snowflakes cascading down towards him. Turning up the collar of his woolen coat, even though he didn't feel in the least cold, he hailed a cab.

This isn't going to be easy, he thought as he watched the large storefront windows in succession pass by with their displays of Rudolph mannequins, elves, Santas, and manger dioramas. *Should I actually take Willa?* he asked himself, the question reverberating with an aura of risk, perhaps peril.

He had met Willa eight months ago, before his transition into GGI. He had accepted an invitation, to an exhibit opening, from one of his painter friends, Lenore, whom he hadn't seen in years. Harkness loved visual art and, as he strolled the gallery, sipping the complimentary wine, he was struck by some of Lenore's paintings, as they reminded him of works by one of his favourites — Joseph Turner. He decided he would purchase those that set fire to his eyes.

"Hey, Jonathan," he heard, recognizing the voice. "Long time, no see," and Lenore came up to him and gave him a big hug.

Lenore was accompanied by a young woman who had long chestnut hair and hazel-coloured eyes.

"This is my friend Willa," Lenore smiled.

The young woman said hello in a slightly demure fashion, and while she momentarily looked off across the gallery as he and Lenore continued to converse, Harkness stole glances at her figure. She was shorter than Harkness, with a small frame. Her upper body was slim and petite and tapered to thighs that flared from her centre in a pleasing heart-shaped manner. She wore a thin cotton shift that slid down her body to her knees, and revealed the contours of her small breasts that hung in an oblique manner from her chest.

"Hi!" Lenore nearly shouted and waved, "Be back in a minute," and left Harkness alone to talk with Willa.

From that day forward, they had become inseparable — he aspiring to the upper echelons of the business class, she an unemployed writer pursuing her imagination through fiction — yet incongruous to their acquaintances. Their bond was unseen by others, a secret world full of lust, desire and compassion for each other. Their sex life was a daily adventure of exploration and uninhibited pleasure, while when their eyes met and their mouths spoke they were full of a deep tenderness and caring, in no way tentative but rather like a force of nature.

Maybe she won't want to go. I'll tell her it's a staid and boring affair — bunch of suits standing around saluting each others' successes, Harkness thought, as he climbed the stairs to their shared condo in a handsome two-storey brownstone.

★

In the basement of Harvest Centre 4, a GGI repository, the laboratory lights had been turned low, the space now vacated by the day's working staff. Only the lone security guard inhabited the place, stationed before the video monitors in his chair in the first-floor reception atrium. Very few, over the next two days, would have occasion to visit the place, since the eve and day of Christmas was a break from activities, and the benefactors had been supplied with their Seasonal fare.

The monitors and the video surveillance apparatus that fed them, mounted throughout the building, were not equipped to transmit other than image. If they had been thus equipped, then perhaps the security man would have picked up on a dripping sound that would've issued from Monitor 14, its camera, slowly panning back and forth, surveying the main laboratory storage area.

The storage area comprised numerous refrigeration units that housed the bounty and wealth of the Corporation. It took up the entire eastern wall of the large open-space laboratory where daily the sorting, classification, testing and sampling occurred; and each container, when finally analyzed and designated for its proper recipient, was stored at the required 4°C to 6°C.

The dripping was an obscene sound. No one likes dripping; especially in a clean and sterile environment.

If the video surveillance unit had been capable of zooming in on the area, this is what it would've seen — Harvest Unit 37's refrigeration door had been neglectfully left ajar (possibly by a distracted technician caught up in his eagerness to get home for Christmas Eve) and a slow viscosity was oozing over the lower edge of the unit, dripping onto the tiled white floor below, providing a startling contrast with its wet scarlet luster. It dripped thusly for nearly an hour.

It came all of a sudden — the refrigeration door blew open, the red viscosity exploding the glass containers within, spewing forth across the white floor in mistletoe patterns, like branching hands reaching into the darkness of the laboratory; but unlike spilt liquid that finds its resting place, the viscous red was asquirm. Its various branched spills sought out each other, snaking together and slowly forming a bulbous mass that grew and grew and grew... and stood eight feet in the air, rivulets of viscosity bubbling and pulsing upward, embryonically evolving into a pattern resembling humanity — it stood, on two legs, with long writhing appendages for arms, two udders distended from its torso leaking a pink milky substance, a stump for a head, eyeless, noseless, but with a large, gaping, toothless mouth that in the moment of its opening gave out a piercing glycerine howl full of needfulness; and without a hesitation, it began tromping towards the laboratory outer door, driven by an internal hunger known only to itself.

★

"You never know," said Willa in a teasing manner, "maybe those boring stiff suits you just mentioned will have their pants stand at attention when they get a load of me."

Willa turned from her armoire-like dresser's mirror, exhibiting the very low-cut translucent beige blouse, under which she wore no bra so her dark nipples were obvious.

She refused to be dissuaded, "I want to see the manner of people you spend most of your day with. I'm sure some of them are as lusty as you," and she laughed.

"Willa?..." Harkness began a protest, but she was upon him before he could continue, her mouth up close to his, her breath warm upon his lips.

"I refuse you to be jealous... I'm the most sexually satisfied woman in the world, what with that pulsing eager dick of yours always following me around. And how's my puppy today?" and she gave a pretend pout as she looked downward.

"Okay," replied Harkness with resignation in his voice, "but, there are some things about the company I haven't mentioned…"

"I'm not squeamish, Jonathan. I know you deal in the blood business. It's competition, right? I bet you've thrown a shadow over the Red Cross," and Willa began to pile things into her purse. "You also mentioned genetic research. That's cutting-edge, breakthrough stuff that could make you rich."

She enveloped him in her arms, pressing her body tightly against his, and kissed him.

"Let's get a cab. Maybe we can get dangerous and, ya know, *play* with each other in the back seat," she said in a low, sultry voice. And so they left.

★

"So where's the little woman tonight, James?" asked Sean Olsen, VP of GGI, as he meandered up to Keats. "I would've thought she'd at least be here for Christmas Eve."

"Worn out. Said she needed a vacation. We're both atheists anyway. This…" and Keats waved his hand towards the lavish buffet that had been set out around the living room, "Christmas stuff is for the employees."

"Well… you folks haven't been getting along very well, so I've heard. Hope things are okay. Nothing serious?" queried Olsen.

Keats looked into Olsen's eyes for some moments, his mind throwing up inchoate images of his twenty-year marriage to Shaya.

"Can I trust you?" he asked Olsen.

Olsen smiled slyly. He liked conspiracies.

"I like the taste of her," and Keats smiled back.

"I understand completely," Olsen laughed out loud, a laugh meant to signify the two of them had just shared a joke, and deflect any conspiratorial aura the others who were milling about may detect.

"Ah, here comes one of our recent recruits," Keats said, suddenly pointing towards the vestibule where Harkness and Willa had just entered.

"See?" whispered Willa as she saw that Olsen was ogling her breasts. "Watch his pants rise to attention," and she giggled.

Harkness ignored her comment and, taking her arm in his, sauntered over to the two Chief Executives of GGI.

There seemed to be good camaraderie in the air as the four chatted aimiably, yet Harkness felt ill-at-ease which he couldn't explain. It wasn't Olsen persistently gazing at Willa's breasts. He felt secure in Willa's affections. Keats was gracious, friendly and was treating Harkness like a son. What was it? It was only when he glanced at the others' hands that he found the source of his anxiety, the others' hands that held glass tumblers full of the rich red liquid. *The wine of life*, Harkness thought to himself, and suddenly felt frightened — not for himself, but for Willa, for her sanity.

"Mr. Keats?" asked Harkness abruptly, "Can we get Willa some wine?"

Keats smiled at Harkness knowingly, "The wine," and Keats stressed these two words, "is over there," and he pointed, "on that sideboard by the French windows."

Relieved, Harkness knew that it would be Burgundy or Chianti, and not what the other two were imbibing. Pouring a glass of wine for Willa, he thought he heard a loud sound from outside. Peering out the window, he noticed a softly falling snow, the street below deserted and dark, but for the single streetlamp.

★

Four days prior, Keats had strode into the Harvest Centre 4 laboratory.

The technician he approached suddenly looked up, "She… I mean, it won't be ready, I'm afraid, for at least another week."

"Can't have it for Christmas Eve?"

"Sorry," replied the technician, "We've had some problems with the genetic coding."

"What kind of problems?" asked Keats.

"The kind of problems that are enigmatic at present, but I'm sure we'll solve them. She… I mean, it, needs a unique solution apparently. A unique cipher, that is. There's something anomalous about one sequence, a sequence that is uncommon. It's not behaving normally."

"Call me when it's ready," said Keats briskly and left.

On his way back to Headquarters, his mind's eye surveyed memories, the memories of a young dark woman, born in Somalia, whose skin had the scent of aeons of dust, whose skin tasted of unripened cheese. She never behaved normally; liked to eat her meat raw; would wipe the blood off her plate with a crust of bread. He admired that. Shaya had aroused him, so he took her away to Toronto, and married her. She had aroused him when she had first disrobed, displaying large, wet, dark-grey labia that hung uncommonly from her vulva, labia that would fill his own mouth with velvety texture, labia on which he would nibble until he drew blood, a sweet ichor! A unique flavour indeed!

★

A soft, gentle snow was falling, and took on a cone formation beneath the streetlight where a teenaged couple loitered. He had his back against the lamppost, while she pressed her body against his, her right leg rubbing up and down his left thigh. They were oblivious to the snow that had settled a fine coat upon their hair and clothing. He was looking down into her eyes, a storm of hot breath between their nearing mouths, when he heard it.

"Dja hear that?" he softly hissed.

"What?" the girl replied, not seeming to pay any heed to his words, her attention more focused on her left hand that was slowly creeping down his belly into his trousers.

He was about to speak when "JAAAM…"came the slurry howl out of a dark corner of the street. Before the girl could react, she felt herself enveloped by a large viscous body, and she knew she was being digested.

The snow continued to fall, silently beneath the street lamp, on to the pavement where there remained only a red smudge, the pavement just outside the home of James Keats.

KALI'S ALPHABET

*From the Journals of Charles Sleeman, Officer of
The Paleontological Society of America*

They told me that, when I had awakened, I had first screamed. Then I began ranting in a language that was neither theirs nor mine. Such was my state of mind that, for some days, I was in delirium — unable to focus on my surroundings, have any awareness of who I was, where I was. Images, sounds, and smells cascaded in a continuous stream overwhelming my senses, and yet none of it was real. Or was it?

When I was able to comprehend their words, they told me that I had been found in sack-cloth lying in the weedy and overgrown back garden of a deserted house. They had assumed I was a vagrant, until they found my wallet, and realized who I was.

They told me my name — Charles Sleeman, and slowly, under their tender administrations, I was able to recover most of my memory, until they bade me farewell.

How had I come to be here, in this small port town of Hanko on the south coast of Finland? This I could not remember. Nor could I remember much of the last few months, the most recent memory being of debarking the ship that had taken me to India where I would begin my excavations.

So I decided to stay in a bed and breakfast, to sojourn a short while in Hanko and commiserate with myself. I needed to explore my suppressed memories, to uncover what I suspected to be dreadful events in my recent history.

★

As the days passed, I wandered the environs, especially the endless beaches and sandy moraines, looking out at the Baltic Sea, walking among pine groves or inspecting the cliff structures along the coastline for fossils. All the time, I was thinking and remembering, reconstructing my past.

I was born in Stratton, Cornwall in 1926, the descendant of a distinguished British family of explorers and adventurers, and son of Francis Sleeman, a forensic chemist who worked closely with Scotland Yard. My great-grandfather was William Henry Sleeman, noted for being the Superintendent of the Thuggee and Dacoity Department in India during British rule, and a major force during his tenure for the elimination of thousands of thuggees. Prior to his military posting in India, he was the first explorer to discover dinosaur fossils in Asia in 1828, which may explain my own love of paleontology.

My mother had died when I was still an infant, so I never knew her. I was reared by my father alone, since there was no other immediate family. He died in 1946, at which point I left England for America where I settled in Salem, Massachusetts. My dream was to become a member of the renowned Paleontological Society, and to hopefully make my mark in history like my great-grandfather before me.

But before I go on, I must talk more about my father. A mystery for me shrouded a part of his life. When a young man pursuing his degree in chemistry, he traveled to India to research various exotic botanicals that would provide him with a pharmacology not familiar to the West. While in Calcutta, he met and fell in love with my mother, Indrani. Throughout my life with him, he refused to talk about her with me. I know, of course, she was Indian, given her name, the colour of my skin and the sole photograph I have of her, found amongst my father's things after his death; but why my father would not tell me of her remains an enigma.

The photograph was taken, I assume, by my father when they were just married, with a backdrop recognizably Calcutta. It shows a young woman, with slightly more than a svelte figure, dressed in a sari and sandals. She has a handsome face, with full lips, an aquiline nose, and perhaps an incongruous feature — bright green eyes, which seem to gain greater intensity from their setting in her dark, brown skin. Something in the photograph, however, was disturbing. At first, I didn't think anything of it, but as I repeatedly looked at the photo, I began to feel unsettled. There was something there I could recognize, but at first refused to interpret — it was her smile. It wasn't normal. Rather than a gentle or carefree or even coy expression, the curvature of the lips and the slightly parted mouth hinted at a lascivious, lustful hunger. The impression was that of an excited predator who knows it has trapped its prey, and is reflecting with pleasure on the coming feast. Looking at the photo in this way, my body began tingling, my skin grew hotter, and the fast pulsing blood in my veins awoke a full erection in my penis, *and this was my mother I was gazing at!*

★

A week had passed, yet still memories of my India expedition remained elusive. I did remember the purpose of the expedition however. Going over the journals of my great-grandfather, William, I had chanced upon some entries related to his discovery of a cult of thuggees situated around Mount Kalanjara in north-central India. This cult was purported to worship the goddess Kali, who has been described as "one of the tongues of Agni," the Hindu god of fire, but is further denoted as "the black tongue of the seven flickering tongues" who "feasts on battlegrounds littered with the dead." In his journal entries, William talked of the difficulties he had in attempting to eradicate the thuggees from this region. The major difficulty being the warren-like system of underground caves that were carved beneath Mount Kalanjara, and that had a complex lattice structure that spread out from the base of the Mount to the surrounding countryside.

While trying, somewhat in vain it appears, to clear the caves of the thuggee vermin, my great-grandfather and his small unit of men happened upon a large cavern, which had been carved out of the rock below the eastern side of Kalanjara. The journal entry is not highly detailed, but what caught my attention was his mention of an altar in the centre of the cavern, upon which had been placed the fossilized remains of some anthropoid creature of prehistory, an "enigma, for the thing obviously had four arms," wrote my great-grandfather. He had wanted to take away the remains, but his small regiment had suddenly found itself under attack and overwhelmed by hundreds of thuggees, and they had to flee the cavern.

This "enigma" fired my imagination and curiosity; so much so, that I proposed to my Paleontological Society an expedition to Kalanjara in search of these fossilized remains. If my great grandfather had been right in his perceptions, then this find would not only explode present anthropological theory, but also open a door onto the unknowable, and perhaps unnamable. The Society accepted my challenge, the requisite arrangements were made, and we set sail for India. The voyage was uneventful. Reaching Calcutta we found suitable accommodations, and there my memories end.

★

It was about the second week of my sojourn in Hanko. I was strolling along the seaside beach in the mid-afternoon when I noticed someone approaching. Even at a distance, I could tell it was a woman, her figure cutting a full-bodied stencil into the air. As she came nearer, I stopped in my tracks, feeling apprehensive for a reason I could not discern.

"Hello," she said as she came up to me and halted.

I replied in kind, but in an almost croaking voice, for I felt somewhat overwhelmed by the vision before me. She was about two metres in height, with skin the colour of dark chocolate. She wore a skimpy shift that revealed long smooth legs, and wore no bra so that her pendulous breasts were distinctly noticeable in contour. Her hair was long and black, reaching down to her broad thighs, and she had startling green eyes.

"I'm Kalma," she said in a deep, smoky and resonant voice.

Rousing myself, as if from a reverie, I replied that I was pleased to meet her, and when I did so, a mischievous twinkle lit her eyes.

"My name is Charles," I somewhat stammered.

"I know," she replied, and smiled in a way that sent a shiver up my spine.

I was at a loss for words. I had never met this woman before, or at least not that I could remember. I started to tremble slightly, the photograph of my mother suddenly in my mind's eye; but this was not my mother.

She then strolled away from me.

"But wait!" I yelled.

"I'll see you later," she called back to me, turning her head in an almost-coy manner, her lips then forming a smile that made my body spasm.

I wanted to run after her, but felt frozen, rooted to the spot, as if some invisible hand held me in check. I watched as she disappeared into a grove of pines. When I finally could move, I felt dizzy, disoriented, as if I had suffered a severe shock. I could do nothing else but collapse into a sitting position upon the sand, and gaze out dazedly at the sea.

★

The sun was slowly setting when I finally came out of my stupor. I arose from the beach, brushed the sand from my trousers, and began walking towards the grove of pines into which Kalma had disappeared. Her name kept echoing in my mind. I felt a strange passion I could not identify, and that would not subside, but seemed to be building obsessively. Her image in my mind's eye had such reality that it seemed to float before me, as if superimposed upon everything in my sight.

I reached the copse of pines and proceeded through. I knew I would not find her, but went on through the woods anyway. When I reached the other side of the grove, I found myself in a clearing which, upon further inspection, turned out to be the Hanko graveyard.

My obsession with Kalma evaporated, for who can step into such a place without placing earthly passions aside? Here the rotting, mouldering corpses of the departed lie; their spirits, wisps of memory in the minds of those still living.

Plaques, tombstones and crypts populated the place. I moved through them, an inner silence having replaced my previous feelings. The graveyard ended at a laneway at the perimeter of town, and, as I was about to exit, I spied a singular crypt set off from everything about it. What caught my attention were the two caryatids framing the tomb's entrance — they both were carved of an obsidian-like stone and had four arms each. I did not stay to reflect on this, but hurriedly made my way back to my room with an intense need for recuperation.

I went to bed early, thoroughly exhausted. For a while I tossed and turned, unable to relinquish the events of the day from my mind. Finally, around midnight, I fell asleep.

★

It's dark, the only light coming from our portable electric lamps. The tunnels are small, so that one needs to crouch slightly in order to proceed. Up ahead I can see Wilson, his back momentarily illuminated by the movement of my lamp. He's on point, having gleaned information from some of the locals about the tunnel system, and on how to reach the central cavern. The other three in our expedition — Jameson, Ryker and Shafely — are behind me, toting the tools and containers for our work.

Wilson, before we entered the tunnels, had related to me the difficulty in getting the information we needed; that the locals feared the warren-like underground of the Mount and would not talk. It was a young boy who, upon hearing Wilson question a resident and spying his Rolex watch, offered the information for the watch. The boy and his friends, despite the admonishment of their elders, would explore the tunnels and caves of the Mount, playing the games that young boys play. They had found the central cavern, but had retreated, the boy expressing that they "hadn't liked the smell."

I could tell we were close to the cavern. There was a foul odour in the air, which increased as we moved ahead. When we finally entered the cavern, the stench was unbearable. We had to soak our kerchiefs in rose-water and wrap them around our mouths.

As our five lamps shone out into the darkness, we stood in stunned silence, Wilson finally speaking.

"How in the hell did they do this?"

The cavern was circular, about a half kilometre in diameter, our crew having estimated this by circumnavigating the walls before moving towards the central area. Its ceiling was so high our lamps could hardly illuminate it, and large thick columns rose to meet that ceiling. What shocked us all was that this cavern was no work of natural forces, but had been carved out of the Mount by human hands.

I was now eager to get to the altar, so I began moving forward towards the cavern's centre, but slowly, since there seemed to be all sorts of odd debris scattered across the floor. I then became confused. When I had reached what I assumed to be the central altar, mentioned in my

great grandfather's journal, I noticed to the right, at some distance, an-
other altar. I proceeded to it, then again noticed yet another altar to its
right. My confusion evaporated when I realized, upon further explo-
ration, that there was a mandala-like arrangement of small altars in
the cavern's centre, in the midst of which rose a larger central one.

My heart now raced as I approached the large altar, and noticed
what appeared to be a heap of stone upon it. Finally, having reached
my goal, I shone my light upon the altar surface. I...

★

... awoke, gasping for breath, my naked body covered in sweat,
my bed linen soaked. Suddenly sitting up in bed, I noticed that
I seemed to have had a nocturnal emission, the hot sperm
splashed across my belly, my penis throbbing, its glans a purplish
red.

My other senses gathered themselves. An aroma wafted
about the room — a musky, aliphatic scent. My tongue seemed
slightly swollen, and there lingered in my mouth an unfamiliar
but distinctly herbal taste.

I then felt certain someone had been in my room. It
seemed they had been able to administer some potion to me
while I slept, one which would keep me unconscious while
they perhaps had their way with me sexually.

I turned on a table lamp and looked about, but found no
trace of another's presence. The door was firmly locked, the
window latch secure.

Feeling shaken and slightly out of breath, I slumped into a
nearby armchair, my gaze unfocused for the moment, then
coming to rest on the large, old fireplace across the room from
where I sat. The room I was renting, on the first floor of the
house in Hanko, had been obviously a family room given the
size of the fireplace, which I estimated to be about one-and-a-
half metres high, and the interior of which could possibly

accommodate a short man. As my gaze came to rest on the hearth, I saw something unexpected. I arose and went towards it. The hearth was comprised of a large flagstone, which had metal hinges on the right side the stone, and a large metallic handle in its middle. Was this some kind of flue to enable a draft into the fireplace, or perhaps a convenient depository for ashes?

I pulled on the handle, the flagstone easily being lifted, and when I looked down, I caught my breath. Before my eyes was the top of a ladder which led down into darkness.

My curiosity was stronger than any fear I felt. After donning some adequate clothing, and retrieving a small flashlight, which I had previously seen in the kitchen, I descended the fireplace ladder.

When I reached bottom, I estimated myself to be about seven or eight metres below ground. Turning on my flashlight, I perceived that I was at the end of a tunnel. It was high and wide enough for a man to walk through with ease. The walls had been overlaid with a darkly stained wood that had strange scratchings upon it, perhaps a language or type of glyph. A draft, which I also had noticed in my descent, came from down the tunnel, and carried with it the musky odour I had encountered in my room. I slowly began walking, inspecting the scratchings as I went.

I don't know how far I traveled, but it felt like a good twenty minutes, before I came to the room. A series of small steps led down from the tunnel into a large chamber. The walls were of a deep amber-coloured wood, and covered with rich ceiling-high tapestries depicting events, perhaps historical, but unfamiliar to me. The floor was covered with oriental carpets of intricate design, their colour full of bright red and deep burgundy.

Throughout the room were various divans, sofas, tables, and pedestals with statues on them. Against one wall was an antique vanity with a sizable mirror, and against another was a circular bed, large enough to provide repose for more than three persons, and with long semi-translucent rose curtains running round it. Along the walls, and between the tapestries, there were other egresses leading from the room alike the one I had just exited. At one interval along the wall farthest from me was a metal door. I moved towards it with an intent of exploring the other side.

As I reached the middle of the chamber, I heard a rustling. Already in a state of apprehension, and something akin to fear, I halted. The sound came from the bed.

"Hello, Charles," came the rich deep voice.

I turned and froze. Kalma slipped from the bed curtains, moving at a languorous pace, her wide hips swaying. She was naked.

"Finally," she said, "you're awake. I wondered how long you'd sleep, and how long it would take you to get here."

With those words, and having reached me, she twined her arms around my waist.

"So good to see you again, and again, and…"

She stopped speaking, and smiled. It was her smile, my mother's smile from the photograph, with its predatory hunger. I let out a small cry.

"Shhh … shhh," and she took my right hand in hers, "it's all right… here take this, drink it… this will calm you."

Moving mechanically, I downed the draft. I knew instantly it was the same as I had tasted previously, and its effects were instantaneous. The room spun. I tried to focus. I felt her arms moving over my body, and I…

★

… called "Wilson, Wilson," while gazing down at the altar top.

"Charles?" he queried, having run to my position, out of breath.

"*Look,*" *I said, the whole frame of my body now shaking.*

Before us, on the altar top, was the fossilized skeleton of a large anthropoid creature over two metres in length. It was obviously female, given the formation of the hips. But it was the arms that bespoke some otherness, an otherness not part of man's evolutionary lineage. Two arms were situated naturally enough, but there were two other arms that grew from behind them out of the shoulder blades.

I was about to speak, when a scream tore through the air. Wilson and I turned instinctively towards it source. But before I could call out to the other members of our group, two other screams erupted in the silence. I began running in the direction from which the initial scream came, leaving Wilson behind. As I reached what I believed to be my destination, I tripped over something, and was sent sprawling, my hands hitting the floor first and encountering a viscous substance. Then another scream echoed in the cavern.

"Wilson!" I shouted, but there was no reply. Raising myself from the floor, I flashed my lamp back in the direction from which I had come, and saw it. Ryker's body, over which I had tripped, was crumpled and twisted, his clothes had been lacerated, his throat slashed, but most horrible of all, his genitals had been torn from him. A blind terror overtook me, and I began running wildly, my only thought being that of escaping, for I knew that my other companions had met a fate similar to Ryker's.

Somehow I found a tunnel leading out of the cavern, and raced down it, hearing, behind me, something in pursuit. I recognized the slap of bare feet on stone, an excited panting and...

★

... coming to consciousness, all sensation was focused on my penis which throbbed from the liquid massage of Kalma's labia. She was astride me on the large circular bed, her thighs slowly moving forward and back, her vulva engorged and pressed against my sex. Her pendulous breasts swung before my mouth, the black nipples erect. I couldn't move. When she saw I was aware, she brought her face up to mine, her large wet red tongue penetrating my mouth for a moment.

I tried to speak, but couldn't.

"It's the drug, Charles," she whispered. One of her hands slowly stroked my face, while another massaged my chest, and with a shock I realized another was caressing my testicles, and yet another played with my glans, even while her soaking wet vulva continued to rub against my erection.

The pleasure mounted and was so intense that I could not feel afraid. I looked into eyes that glittered a brilliant green, and she smiled my mother's smile from the photograph. She began to hiss, and then moved her thighs so that my penis slipped into her burning vagina. Our genitals undulated, and I felt a hunger spread throughout my body.

Gasping, she began to chant, "Sahodara, sahodara... oh my sahodara."

I repeated her chant, not knowing what it meant, the pleasure and hunger becoming extreme, until my penis erupted, the hot sperm splashing the walls of her vagina. She, feeling my orgasm, hissed as she swooned into her own, her vagina suddenly becoming like a mouth sucking at my penis, sucking forcefully all my sperm up into her womb.

I lay exhausted and paralysed.

Kalma arose from her postion astride me, and walked to the vanity with the large ovular mirror. While I couldn't move my head, my eyes were able to follow her, and I saw some of my sperm oozing down her inner right thigh. She sat before the vanity, took a brush, and began combing out her long black hair.

"Mother would be proud of you," she said, her eyes meeting mine through the mirror.

I felt a tremor shake my body. I tried to reply, but was unsuccessful.

"You've remembered haven't you?" she asked rhetorically, "I'm sorry about your colleagues, but I was able to save you. My minions had other plans for you, but it was fortunate that you ran as you did, with me as your pursuer." She arose from the vanity, went to a small table, and poured liquid into a small vial-like glass, before coming to where I lay.

Looking down at me, she continued, "I brought you here to Hanko. This is my realm, and you will be safe here. I needed you, your body, your essence, so that we could continue our line," and saying this she held out all four of her arms towards me. "I'm sorry I left you as I did, but you needed time to mend and be cared for by others. Drink this. It will allow you to sleep," and she poured a small amount of liquid into my mouth.

I stared into her green eyes, and thoughts rampaged through my brain, too fantastical and intolerable to contemplate; and as I began my slip into unconsciousness, I heard her final whisper, which held an unexpected tenderness, as she said "Sleep now, my love, and, if you wish it, we will meet again at a future time."

★

When I awoke, she was gone. I climbed from the bed, and found my clothes. Donning them, I tried not to think of what had transpired.

Averse, for some fearful reason, to wending my way back through the tunnel whence I had come, I decided upon the metal door I had noticed upon entry into the room. Pulling it open, I was assaulted by a strong odour of must and decay, and realized with horror, as I stepped through the door, that I was in a small crypt, the walls of which were lined with sarcophagi. Without thinking, I rushed across the floor to what I presumed was the exit to outdoors. Relief flooded me as I stepped out into the air and daylight. I knew where I was — in the Hanko graveyard. Walking away, in the direction towards my rented room, I happened to glance back. I saw the crypt I had exited, the crypt with the two caryatids.

It has been a year now, since I returned to my home in Salem, and she has not appeared. The past events seem to me as a dream, and I've begun to believe that they had all been part of a severe delirium. Yet I can't help but confront the fact that my expedition colleagues were never heard of again, that the word "sahodara" comes from the Sanskrit and means "brother," and that a photograph appeared afterwards on a table in my room in Hanko, a picture of my mother with two babies, cradled within her four arms.

It was many years after his father's death in 1829, during one of his dreadful bouts of depression, that my friend Joseph had delivered to me, by boy courier, a short note that simply read:

"Must see you immediately. Meet me at the Red Lion in Whitehall. Be discreet. Do not let any one know of this meeting."

Now I must tell you, this was upsetting for me. I had been worried about Joseph ever since he'd disappeared three months ago. At the time, I thought he had simply gone on one of his excursions to the mainland without telling any of his friends or acquaintances, Venice being one of his decidedly special places to sojourn with his own spirit. Yet now, with such a short and cryptic communiqué, and coming from here in London itself, I began to have an unsettling suspicion that Joseph had fallen into some unsavoury business, perhaps with one of those lower-class women with whom he was wont to discreetly cavort, and occasionally become obsessed with.

My friend... what transpired, however, was so terrible, so utterly beyond my psyche's abilities to encompass as reality — at least, the reality we all agree upon and get on with in the day-to-day — that I am surprised I did not end up in the madhouse.

I will tell you what happened, only in confidence, mind you, but first some background as to how I came to be both financial supporter and friend of the notable Joseph Mallord William Turner. Here, have another glass of ale.

★

I am, you may say, an appreciative collector of fine art, and I have at my hand a considerable amount of disposable income, left to me by my late parents. In this regard, it came naturally to me to invest in what I love most — the glorious images of teeming life and nature around us, created and captured by those visionaries who wield the painter's tools — and to invest not only in the physical objets d'arts themselves, but also to be able to give support to those I felt worthy, those who were on the cutting edge of their art, producing beauty and at the same time challenging it, yet at times finding themselves struggling to survive financially.

So it was not unusual, having gone on a tour of small galleries throughout southern England, that I would happen upon a rumour of a private exhibition of paintings to be displayed at Pentworth House, the estate of George Wyndham, Third Earl of Egremont, situated in West Sussex. Having many dignified friends in the area, it was no difficulty in establishing an invitation to the exhibition.

I won't bother you, my friend, with all the cumbersome details of my visit there — my distinguished hosts, their splendorous heritage, the plethora of foods and beverages they made available to their guests — but come more to the point, since my visit was to inspect the new paintings by the heralded young artist Joseph Turner.

Upon entering the hall that the Wyndhams had reserved for the exhibition, I suddenly felt a strange giddiness without knowing from what it arose. Somehow, in the casual and momentary glance that I had cast upon the room of paintings, it was as if my eyes had become full of light, as if a hundred sunrises and sunsets had burst upon my vision simultaneously, the paintings seeming to glow with an internal luminance, and I found myself being drawn towards them as if I were a somnambulant with a destination circumscribed by dreams. Shipwrecks, fires, natural catastrophes — all the images represented in paint glowed and seemed lit from within.

Thus I found myself standing in front of one of those glowing visions — a painting, to be sure, and depicting a shipwreck during a violent storm, but one which confronted and shattered all of my habitual perspectives on what I had thought of as art. Here was a chromatic palette I had never encountered, one in which broadly applied washes of paint created an ephemeral atmosphere with a luminous transparency that was not possible with oil paint. It was as if the artist had conspired with some ethereal alchemy to turn oil into tempera, such was the lightness and fluency of the painting.

"Does it appeal to you?" — these words spoken and entering my consciousness as if from a distant world. Slowly I turned from the painting and found myself looking at a young man with well-trimmed hair the colour of dust, large dark eyes over which large dark eyebrows hovered, his long face ending with a pleasant mouth above a sharp chin, and a prominent long nose quite wide for such a long face.

"Yes," I said, "very much so."

"I'm Joseph Turner, and these are my paintings," he said quite casually, with no pretensions whatsoever.

"How have you done this, and in oils!" I sputtered.

A pleased glint appeared in his eyes as he replied, "Here, let's get a glass of wine and I'll tell you."

★

So my friend, that was my first meeting with him, and over the decades our acquaintance grew into a friendship that was both emotionally and aesthetically rich and satisfying. Of course, Joseph was not as well situated as I, so when the need arose I could support him financially, specifically by purchasing those sublime visions he created on canvas, and in other times simply by providing him with some pocket money for a night on the town.

There's no need to go into the details of our friendship and history together, nor his meteoric rise to acclaim as one of

Britain's foremost avant-garde artists. Rather, my friend, I need now to tell you of what transpired after I received that unusual note from Joseph that I mentioned at the beginning of our conversation.

★

I went to meet him at the Red Lion as he had directed. I knew right away something was desperately wrong — for one, he ignored my request to order drinks, and immediately launched into an explanation of where he had been the last many months. Still feeling, after all these years, totally despondent from the death of his father — and I must mention here that father and son had a special bond, so much so that his father became his studio assistant for some time before his demise — Joseph felt the need to escape, escape his friends, his acquaintances, idolators, critics, et cetera.

"It's in Whitechapel," he said. As I looked at him, he appeared a different creature — his face gaunt, hair unkempt, clothes shabby, and his eyes never still, darting this way and that as if a fearful vigilance had overtaken him, as if he were hunted prey.

"I need you to come with me. I need to show you something. I know what you're thinking, but for friendship's sake, I'm in dire need of you," and with those words spoken, I could not resist. Here was someone as dear to my heart as anyone would be. I could not forsake him... but, God forbid — Whitechapel?

As we went our way, I could not quite accept our destination. Here was my good friend, both distinguished and erudite in the arts, leading me to perhaps one of the most despairing parts of London, a neighbourhood full of cutthroats, prostitutes and any manner of low-life, all of whom lived within squalour amid dilapidated, decaying and foul living quarters. But for the occasional greasy pub, poor shops offering mostly worn wares, and fishmongers, the area was a dense rat's nest.

"I had to get away," he spoke to me in a feverish manner. "What with father gone so long and everything, I felt I had to do something different."

"But my boy," I began, but he interrupted.

"I found this place, this house — yes, I know, it's not what you would expect of me. I rented it, the whole property. It's called Blacking House. The landlord was, as you would expect, overjoyed even though suspicious, but turned a blind eye. He could see I came from the outside, that I was not a denizen of Whitechapel."

I did not say anything.

"I heard about it from an acquaintance," he was saying as we neared the area. "He told me it had a wonderful loft on the second storey, with wall-to-ceiling windows and a southern exposure. How could I resist. It would be ideal for... well, new work."

We walked on. All around us were houses, houses with dark doorways where occasionally you would spot one of them — heavy make-up barely concealing the scars of some disease ravishing them from the inside, some with red or purplish boils erupting on their faces, all of them smoking, calling, cajoling, trying to catch your eye. The houses themselves were anomalies, since gravity should have torn them down long ago, and the stench — of urine, stale tobacco, rotten vegetables and fruit thrown on to the street from overhead windows, and a dead dog rotting in a gully — was practically unbearable.

Joseph suddenly took my arm. "It's up here," as he led me up a narrow alley so dark I found it hard to see, until my eyes adjusted, and then saw we had reached a dead end, a wall with a simple door, somewhat worm-eaten and painted red, the paint having flaked over the years, leaving patterns down the door as if some creature had clawed it from top to bottom.

★

I must admit I was somewhat surprised when we entered the abode to find it relatively well-kept, not dirty nor moldy, yet with an unmistakable smell of must and decay. From a narrow, partially lit hallway, he led me to a staircase that we ascended to the rooms above, and then to a door along a landing which he opened and bade me enter.

I entered into darkness, he shuffling past me and lighting the many oil lamps he had set around the room. It was his studio, relatively spacious, with the large windows he had mentioned facing south.

"Have some brandy," he said, and quickly poured each of us a thumb's-worth in small glasses and, after having given me mine, proceeded to scrape a wooden chair across the room, which he then seemed to place strategically.

"Please, sit," he asked.

I did so, and suddenly perceived directly in front of me an easel which had been draped over with a white coarse linen sheet.

"I've something to show you. It's a painting, of course, but different from what I've done in the past." He said this in a rather agitated manner. "Another direction perhaps," he continued, "and I... I... need your honest assessment. I need you to be my friend, to tell me whether or not I'm going mad," and without letting me respond in any manner, he tore the sheet from the easel.

I must tell you, I felt somewhat bewildered at first, primarily because I was expecting my eyes to be met with one of those luminous visions, one of those paintings full of fire and motion. What I perceived instead was a darkling image overall. Creeping from all edges of the canvas toward the centre was darkness. Only in the centre of the canvas did an image dully glow. At first impression, it reminded me of some of those ancient portrait paintings by Rembrandt, the master of light and darkness, where the central illuminated figure seemed literally to jump out of the darkness; but as I continued to gaze at the canvas, I realized that the dim luminosity that existed in the painting was meant only to reveal the central image by stealth, as if the image itself did not want to be realized, but to hide in the shadows. Gone was the swirling, atmospheric impressionism born from my friend's avant-garde techniques. Here instead was a naturalistic, or should I say, photographic representation.

I turned to my friend. "Joseph," I said, "what is this? As far as I can tell, it's a rather ordinary picture of, if I'm not mistaken, a type of trap door set in a floor."

Joseph had been silent and staring at me all the while I had been assessing the painting.

"It's in the cellar..." he said faintly, almost in a whisper, continuing to stare at me, "in the cellar of this place. I found it. I can show you."

"But Joseph," I sputtered, "this... this isn't art, this... it's mere representation. What on earth have you done? Why this? This isn't like you at all. Your gift, your wonderful gift... I don't see any evidence of the artist I know in this... this..." I couldn't continue, feeling betrayed, all the admiration, appreciation that had manifested itself around those visionary paintings of his, now absent. Catching my breath, and somewhat harshly to my friend saying, "This is no new direction, Joseph. This is devolution, a step backwards... what on earth are you thinking?"

His countenance seemed to sag, then he looked up at me.

"I know," he said, "but I had to say something to get you here," then suddenly his eyes seemed to blaze. "Listen, listen carefully to what I'm going to tell you. I painted that," and he gestured towards the canvas, "as a document. That door, it's real enough, and as I've said, it's below us."

He then took a deep breath. "Something comes... something comes out of that door... at night it comes, only at night. I can hear it... hear it moving about the house, the first floor, never venturing up here." He took another deep breath. "I haven't seen it, but... it's left prints, footprints... so you see, there's something... something living beneath the cellar of this house, and I don't think it's human, because... well you see... the footprints, they look human, but... they're very large, and... there're six toes, do you understand, six toes on those feet," and he stopped, his eyes having moved away from me and now staring at the canvas.

★

Well, let me tell you, I found myself in an incredulous state, and for the first time entertained the thought that perhaps my friend had gone mad, perhaps the strain of being on the edge of his art, the strain of continually challenging his creative powers that gave birth to those groundbreaking visions in paint, had finally eroded his nervous system and led to mental collapse.

"I can see it in your face," he said despondently. "You think I'm fit for the madhouse, but I'm not insane, I swear, and if there was only some way I could prove to you that..."

At that point, I interrupted, having just had an idea. "Look," I said, "let's say you're right. You say this apparition, this creature, whatever it is, only comes up at night. Perhaps therefore it has an aversion to daylight. I suggest then, that to prove to me and to yourself that this is a figment of your imagination, probably brought on by acute stress, that we go down there now. We'll go and inspect the place thoroughly."

A look of vast relief flooded Joseph's whole being. "I was hoping for something like this. I knew if you came, and being my good friend, you would help," he said, for while Joseph was of a delicate nature, there was no lack of fortitude or courage in him, those qualities that had enabled him to challenge our very perceptions of art and reality.

So, after each of us had quaffed a hearty glass of brandy, we began our descent to the cellar, picking up, on our way, two adequately filled oil lamps and some matches.

★

Lighting our oil lamps, we entered the cellar down a narrow stair that led to a dirt floor. The ceiling was high and the place was empty but for an old rag or two that had been tossed in a corner. At the far end of the cellar, from where we had entered, was the trap door, practically level with the dirt floor. It was painted in the same red as was the front door of the house, but what surprised me… you see, in Joseph's painting, one could not get the proper perspective as to its dimensions… was its size. It was a good twelve feet square. It had an iron ring attached to one end, the means by which one would pull the door upward and open.

Joseph and I looked at each other, and we didn't need to speak. We both knew what we would do. Pulling together, we hoisted open the portal, and gazed upon a stair, but not a stair made of wood — rather a stone stair having been noticeably and crudely carved out of the rock firmament below the house. Without a word, but both of us admittedly feeling some trepidation, we descended.

The stair went down, went down in my estimate a good thirty feet below ground.

"My god," I let out, but Joseph remained silent.

Upon reaching bottom, we both stopped, and found ourselves in a kind of stupour as we gazed before us. We were in a kind of antechamber, semi-circular, acting both as, I assumed, an entrance and exit room. For going off in different directions were passageways: two leading off to the extreme right and left, two more going off on 45° angles, and one directly in front of us. My mind reeled. Nowhere had I ever read or heard of such a thing — a series of tunnels carved out of the bedrock below London? Perhaps smugglers or pirates had created these to evade the law; but, as far as I knew, there was no record of such a thing.

I glanced at my friend, and said, "This changes things."

He looked at me, "Which way?"

Both of us then looked straight ahead, and began slowly walking.

★

We had gone some ways, perhaps a quarter of a mile, when we spotted a light up ahead. There was no sound except for the soft sounds of our footsteps, but we proceeded cautiously. Upon exiting the passageway, we found ourselves within a circular room, which we noted had been recently inhabited, and had two other passages, apart from the one from which we had come, leading off in other directions. Sparsely furnished, the room held a few old dilapidated wooden chairs, a large similar-type table, a few chests, and a large pile of straw with moth-eaten woolen black blankets strewn over top, apparently to accommodate rest or sleep.

The room was lit with large tapers that sat within recesses cut into the walls. The stench made us both gag and put our sleeves to our faces. I looked at my friend. He was visibly shaking, his eyes bulging, staring at a section of the floor.

I gasped, as my eyes beheld what his had already encountered.

There before us strewn in various areas on the floor were the remnants of what I assumed to be carcasses, or more correctly, parts of carcasses, and not just flesh and bone, but entrails, and as my eyes took in more, God forbid, they were recognizable as human.

"We must go," I whispered urgently, grasping my friend's sleeve, for my eyes had spotted various cutting utensils scattered across the surface of the large table, as well as the large redbrown stains that had pooled and clotted there, and as I turned towards our egress, the passage from which we had come, I heard it — a slow shuffling of feet — but I could not determine the direction from which the sound came. Was it one of the other two passages that led off the room, or the passage we had come from, so disorienting were the acoustics of the place…

… and when Joseph's ears finally registered the shuffling noise, he inadvertently let out a small shriek, but not so small as to not alert whatever was coming towards us, because the shuffling turned into a clopping, much like the sound of a horse, which was accompanied by a type of liquid howl issued from who knew what kind of mouth.

Grabbing my friend's arm, I took the chance, and raced back the way we had come, my friend following as quickly, offering no resistance.

We exited the passageway, exited the antechamber, not thinking to stop or look back, exited the cellar and exited Blacking House itself, never, God forbid, to return.

★

So my friend, that is my story.

I refuse even to this day to speculate upon my experience, since it has been more important to me to put it out of my mind, and to attend to Joseph. We have never talked about it, yet I have kept a constant vigilance about him, for he still suffers those terrible bouts of depression, and through my encouragement and affection he has returned to his true calling, has begun once more to create those visions in paint, those luminous visions that raise our spirits and dispel the darkness that creeps, creeps about at the corners of our world.

SOURCE ACROSS SOMA

My dearest friend,

How I miss you. I'm writing this letter in the hope that it will dispel within your self any notion that I am an evil man. We had very little contact during the time of which I write, so I wish to allay any insidious rumours about me you may have encountered, and present my case before you.

It has been two years since I came to this place seeking refuge, needing to put time and space between myself and the world, to allow the memory of my name and the events surrounding me to evaporate in the minds of men. Yet even here in this sheltered sanctum, where the walls are thick, and the metal doors easily sealed with strong latches, I do not feel at ease, knowing what I know now, knowing that the events I caused and their reverberation may be irreversible, events that through some karmic vengeance may be, at this moment, about to descend upon me.

You know, of course, of my intense research in cognitive psychophysiology, and my famed stature, among my colleagues, in the overall field of neuroscience. As well, I'm sure you'll remember, my eccentric passion for macabre literature, since many a night you and I would discuss the writings of Poe or Lovecraft, reveling in the psychological insights we believed we uncovered in their works.

What you're unaware of, however, is how that eccentric passion spiraled into the applied research I had been conducting at the University, and how this unlikely union led to experiments that opened a door, a portal in the mind, through which a palpable, yet unnameable horror, could enter our reality.

★

It was just before March break of that year at the University, when I approached a number of my students, asking them if they would all stay on over the break, and aid me in new research. There were five of them and, in their eagerness and excitement at my offer, they all agreed, since they were still at the stage of their theoretical studies, and had yet to do any applied science.

I had set up a private laboratory off-campus, since the unorthodox nature of my research would have surely upset my colleagues if they came surreptitiously nosing about my work. My students, however, had fresh, open minds, not prejudiced by any set of conventional theories or knowledge that can ensnare the myopic academic.

As a preliminary, I met with my students over a two-day period, outlining and then detailing the course our research would take. I talked about aspects of psychometry, especially the phenomenon of astral projection, reading to them from Colin Wilson's comprehensive tome, *The Occult*. I also provided them with research papers by distinguished scientists who were working in the field of genetic memory.

My goal, I explained, was to reach what I termed as The Source — another dimension existing beyond the veil of our consensual reality, and from which, I believed, all existence originated. We would use sleep induction, and resulting dream-states, coupled with a powerful hallucinogen, to reach our goal. The hallucinogen, called soma, was a beverage made from the juice of a plant that certain Hindu cults had used in their Vedic ritual sacrifices and offerings to the gods. Two of the students, Jonathan and Kyla, would be the subjects; the other three — Brady, Jeffrey, and Heather, along with myself, would act as guides and monitors. The first stage of the experiment would involve the two subjects in intense exercises which would discipline their minds, and that would focus their thoughts and feelings like a laser beam. In this way, they would have the strength of willpower to navigate the wayward dream states and effects of the hallucinogen.

Once I felt the students to be fully briefed, I introduced them to my off-campus laboratory. It was a good-sized room in the basement of a house, which I had rented, just a few short blocks from the University. I had spent the previous year filling and arranging the room with the scientific equipment I would need for my experiments. The prime focus in the lab was what I termed The Bath. It comprised a large tub of about three metres in length, one metre wide, and one metre in depth. The tub was filled with a special saline solution, which would allow a body to float practically on its surface. Situated strategically around it were various machines, such as electrocardiographs, electrocephalographs, and a magnetic resonance imager, all of which were attached to a computer network with four monitoring stations. Given that my students were also studying medicine, they had a working knowledge of this equipment. So the first day was taken up with testing the machinery, and preparing The Bath, before we left in the evening to get rest prior to the first experiment, which was to be early the next morning.

*

It was Kyla who volunteered to be the first subject. She was short in stature, and fairly attractive, with blue eyes and red hair. Full-bodied, she was somewhat plump. When I told her she would have to be naked, she brushed my comment aside, and began undressing. I couldn't help but admire her large, firm breasts, and after some good-natured sexual banter between her and the young men, she slipped into The Bath. I had her drink a small vial of the soma drug, before she lay back and began floating, and then busied myself with attaching the various monitor electrodes to her head and torso. When she had fallen asleep, the rest of us manned our computer stations, and began our vigil.

Three hours passed, as we monitored her vital signs which remained steady throughout. It was when I was inspecting her brain patterns through the MRI scan that I noticed above normal activity, and suddenly heard the first splashing sounds. We all rushed to The Bath, where Kyla's body was convulsing, the saline solution sloshing over the sides of the tub. I tore the electrodes from her skin, and three of us lifted her out. Her eyes were open, but the eyeballs were curled up into her skull and showed only their whites. We got her on her feet, and then Heather yelped and pointed. Between Kyla's legs, from her vulva, there poured forth a torrent of female ejaculate and urine. One of the boys ran for towels. In bewilderment, I gazed at her body, a body that had grown considerably thinner, her breasts being deflated and half their normal size, and in shock I saw the milk begin dribbling from her erect nipples as if some invisible mouth was suckling them. Gobs of saliva and mucus began flowing from her mouth and nose respectively. Grabbing the towels that Brady had rushed back with, we all began mopping and wiping her body. I felt helpless as the liquids continued to gush out of her. Finally it abated, along with her convulsions. We carried her gingerly to a nearby sofa, covering her with dry towels.

I kept repeating her name until her eyes opened, and then she let out a scream that should not issue from the mouth of any human being. We all crouched around her, trying to soothe her, our own nerves jangled and frayed. She finally became sufficiently calm to tell us what she had experienced, though at times she began sobbing, and this is what she related:

"My first recollection was of being in a boat, a small flat-bottomed vessel, that had its own animation and locomotion, for it was sailing upon the water with no aid from me. I was alone in the boat. I scanned the horizon, but could discern no land. Some time passed, and then I saw it. Very slowly, something began emerging from the water. At first, I was afraid, until I recognized that it was a small island rising out the sea. There seemed to be what looked like stone ruins upon the land, and I then noticed that my boat had veered and was now traveling towards the isle.

"As my boat neared land, a thick, shroud-like mist began to collect in the air, and as I stepped from the vessel, I felt it envelope me. I began walking towards what I now knew were ruins, the remnants of some large, ancient architecture, which had, over time, tumbled down. My purpose now was to inspect this site, and perhaps learn of the place, but as I walked towards it, the mist grew thicker such that I felt I was moving through some viscous substance and, to my concern, felt as if the mist were caressing my skin.

"I had just reached the foot of the tumbled ruins, when it happened. I watched in horror as the mist took the form of large hands, which proceeded to grab on to my breasts, and as I realized that I was naked, I felt something long and thick penetrate my vagina. Fear coursed through me, but was then replaced with a raging lust. The thing in my vagina began pulsing violently, and rather than the sensation that comes from fucking, the inward and outward motion of a penis, it felt like the thing was sucking at my insides. Then I knew, even amidst the explosive orgasm I could not avoid, that I was being drained. My vital energy was being sucked from me, and I grew more thirsty every moment. Then I heard a voice, your voice, calling my name," and Kyla looked at me. Then, very slowly, she pulled down the towel which covered her chest, and looked at her breasts which, having been firm and somewhat perky, now hung pendulously. She proceeded to inspect her body, scanning the thinness of her arms and legs. Looking back up at me, and through tears, she said, "Well, I guess now I've got the svelte figure I always wanted."

★

I sent Jeffrey away to get food and fruit juices, and when he returned Heather began feeding Kyla, and the rest of us ate and drank as well.

I proposed ending the experiment, but met with resistance. Even though something horrific had happened, and one of our team had been physically and emotionally traumatized, they all wanted to continue. They all knew that we had reached our goal, yet did not understand what this meant. Did Kyla actually astral travel to a physical destination in another dimension where she encountered some vampiric being, or were her bodily manifestations and changes due to some unknown, immanent psychic force that had been unleashed? Kyla herself, despite her experience, was adamant that we proceed, feeling that since she had sacrificed a considerable part of herself, then at least she had a right to know what had really happened.

In having stocked the laboratory, I had brought in six small sofas which would roll out into beds. If our research demanded a long concentrated effort, we may not be able to interrupt it, and, in all likelihood, would need to live in the lab.

With some reluctance, I conceded to my students' wish to pursue what we all now felt to be a groundbreaking discovery, but suggested that we rest, sleep and nourish ourselves, before continuing the next day.

Before retiring, Kyla approached me.

"Thank you," she said, "for calling me back," and she smiled warmly.

I looked at her, and though she had grown thinner, I saw she once again wore the healthy glow of a young, passionate woman.

★

In the morning, it was decided that Kyla would no longer play the role of subject, but we would try again, this time with Jonathan.

Being over two metres in height, and despite his pursuit of a career in neuroscience, Jonathan had the body of an athlete. When he had taken off his clothing in preparation for The Bath, Heather, dressed in a light, short dress, had let out a soft whistle, as she gazed at his long, husky penis.

Knowing his strength and stamina, I still felt a foreboding, and therefore told Jonathan I would waken him at any sign of physical distress. He slipped into the bath, and I administered the drug and electrodes. When he was finally asleep, I brought a chair over beside the tub, and sat watching him. Kyla now manned the MRI.

I don't know how much time passed, for I had negligently nodded off, and was only roused when I heard a shout. My eyes beheld the thrashing, convulsing form of Jonathan, before being thrown back from my chair on to the floor. His body had bolted up out of the tub, and in doing so had collided with me. Fearing that what had happened to Kyla would now overtake Jonathan, I quickly gained my feet, my intention being to go to his aid. I looked to the others, and saw they were frozen in terror. My sight shot back to Jonathan, and then I froze too.

Before me was Jonathan's hulking form. The entire surface of his skin was rippling like disturbed water, and was turning black. I saw a mist begin to exit from all his orifices, as his muscular and skeletal structure began to warp and tumesce. I yelled to Heather, who was standing but two metres in front of him, but she couldn't respond, so rooted to the spot in terror was she. I was about to run to her, when I was shocked into immobility by what I witnessed. In helpless horror, I saw a spectacle that would haunt me all my days.

It was Jonathan's penis, which grew at a tremendous speed, and sought its target in Heather who stood metres away. Within seconds it had traversed the distance between them, found its way up her skirt, ripped through her panties, and penetrated her vagina. The terrified look on the girl's face suddenly twisted with pain, then transformed into the face of hungry lust. I stood there transfixed in terror and disgust, as she was slowly lifted off the ground, and then hung like a puppet, impaled upon the penis.

I suddenly howled when the loud sucking noise began. I saw Heather's body begin to crumble inwards, watched her matter being ingested, and travel in large lumps inside and along the penis back to the hulking form which had become unrecognizable and obscene.

I ran at the thing, but some part of it struck out, throwing me across the room into a set of large shelves, which collapsed and buried me. I lost consciousness. When I came to, the laboratory was in flames. I staggered about looking for the members of my team, but only found four skeletons.

★

My friend, I fled as far away as I could, and found this sanctuary. It is high in the mountains of Nepal. So I wait, for that is all that is left to me — waiting. At times, I freeze in terror, thinking I'm hearing, from outside my room, that obscene sound, that loud sucking. My only hope now is that you'll receive this letter, before it finds me, before it finds you.

Your friend,

H.

Richler moves sluggishly in his chair, slowly swivels it, looks at Kardov.

"Nothing," he says.

"What did you expect?" his co-pilot replies, Kardov intent upon completing a crossword puzzle.

"But it's only a day away, and you'd think they'd be in contact, give us further orders, perhaps even ask us what we see." Richler swivels in his chair again, peers through the macroscopic digital display. "I mean… we're almost there."

Kardov ignores Richler's comments, grunts, rises while throwing aside his palm-gamer — "Must be interference… lotsa stuff now between us and them." He moves towards the nourishment compartment — "Wanna beer?"

Richler thinks — *You make a history of yourself; you can't help it — seeing yourself reflected back in time. Here I am over my prime — look at the salt and pepper growth issuing from my upper lip and chin! You make a history of yourself, don't you — but who will remember if they can't hear us, or if they don't want to hear us, don't want to know what we find, what we discover?*

"You're getting anxious again, ya always get anxious, yet ya know this has always been a one-way trip… so have a beer," Kardov filling two glasses with a red ale from the nourisher. "Ya think too much — because ya see too much. Stop seeing and just observe." Placing a glass of red ale beside Richler, he returns to his palm-gamer and the unfinished crossword.

Richler looks at the red ale, watches the effervescence of the gaseous substance froth up and leave bubbles clinging to the inside of the glass. "Look," he says, "then why are we all the way out here if they're not interested in what we're about to discover?"

"Discover?" Kardov takes a deep drink of his draft. "I know what ya think you want to discover… but you rebellious scientific types just won't give it a rest, will ya? I mean, what's wrong with the Big Bang anyway? Lots of ya think that's the answer… but NOOO — you think otherwise. Okay, so you're not a navel-gazer like so many of your colleagues… but even if ya think ya know you're right, when ya discover it, it won't matter, in a matter of time you'll be dead."

"Thanks for the ale," says Richler, continuing to gaze into the digital display. Seeing nothing new, he relaxes, thinks of how many years have passed, how many decades… *Why wouldn't they want to know?*

★

Out here there aren't any stars — the stars are behind you — they've stopped moving for you.

★

Time has stopped — Richler looks at the millennium clock, takes a drink of ale, is afraid of thinking, turns to Kardov… "There's no more time."

"You've been ogling that thing far too long," says Kardov from his bunk, sleepy eyes trying to make out his pilot's position. "There's always time… always."

"The clock's stopped," says Richler, raising his glass of ale to Kardov in a mock salute.

"Maybe it's broken," Kardov says glibly, slowly getting up and shuffling over to the digital display, playing with the switches for the clock's settings. "It's not broken…" slowly turning his gaze to Richler, "… what the hell?"

At the precise moment of the uttered word "hell," the ship jerks, shudders and comes to a stop.

"We must be there," Richler whispers, a look of awe spreading across his face.

"Let's go to observation," Kardov's voice now sounding uncertain, perhaps fearful, yet determined. Both men move mechanically to the vaculator which will transport them to the upper level observation deck.

The deck is at the prow of the ship, but somewhat recessed from the nose, and is semi-circular, the walls comprising floor to ceiling windows protected from the outside with titanium shutters that slide down into the ship when one wishes to view the 180° vista ahead.

It is pitch black until Kardov switches on the dim glow lights, Richler proceeding to the console with the shutter controls. He presses a button and the shutters silently and slowly fall into the floor.

At first, all the two men perceive is thorough blackness, so dense that it seems palpable like a solid wall of tar.

"Well?" Kardov more to himself than Richler, "There's nothing there."

Richler pushes another button on the console, and the large headlights on the prow of the ship blaze to life, and as they do so the eyes of both men fill with an image, an image familiar, an image that shouldn't be there — both men are staring, not knowing what to think, their emotions cascading through a repertoire including fear, surprise, awe and confusion — both men are staring at what seems to be the prow of their ship.

After about a minute, Richler manages to compose himself and focus his thought. "It's like we're looking into a gigantic mirror, and seeing ourselves reflected back."

Both men have moved right up to the windows and can see themselves standing out there on the observation deck of the ship, the other ship.

"It's not a mirror," Kardov says, "it's a goddam reflective barrier or membrane of some sort..."

"Okay, wait," says Richler, beginning to formulate within himself the reason for his being here, for having spent a lifetime traveling across the interstellar void, for having ideas contrary to the accepted ones of his time — that the universe began from nothing in an explosion that spewed out gases and matter, nebulae and galaxies, hurled out from the focal point of the explosion, hurled out (as far as mankind could discern) towards infinity, and that there was nothing else out there beyond the traveling edge of their own universe, nothing, an infinite nothingness. "Kardov, if there's a barrier, then there's something on the other side of the barrier..." Richler letting his comment sink into Kardov's mind.

"What the hell are ya talkin' about?" Kardov's voice low and tentative.

Richler replying, "Okay, look — mankind has believed for some time that the universe began with a bang and moved outward towards an infinite nothingness, and that eventually the universal motion would slow and finally stop, and the universe would slowly fizzle out and freeze in the interstellar void — but, here's the thing — it hasn't stopped yet, and in fact it has enough velocity left in it to reach this point we're at now, and..." his voice hesitating, as he looks at Kardov; Kardov suddenly turning his head towards Richler, astonishment in his eyes, "and the goddam universe is gonna smash right into this, this dead end, this barrier thing," Kardov's voice alive with recognition.

★

The two men sat at a table back in their living quarters, full pints of red ale being quaffed slowly one after another.

"What do we do now?" Kardov was the first to speak, a stunned silence having followed them back from the observation deck.

Richler took a long drink from his stein. "I think, first, we send back a report, tell them what we've found, and then..." Richler taking another deep drink, "... and then, we continue."

Kardov stared at him, his mouth having fallen open. "What the hell! Continue where? It ends here, the universe ends here. There's nowhere to go. Are ya daft?"

"We'll *try* to continue," Richler's whole body becoming animated. "We'll use the forward rockets and see if we can blast a hole through the barrier, put a gaping fissure in that dead-end wall of yours, and if we can, then we'll continue through and see what's on the other side. Come on, we'll go to forward command," and with that Richler leapt from his chair, motioning Kardov to come with him with the hand carrying his stein of red ale.

★

"This is nuts," Kardov at his console readying the forward rockets for launch, while Richler seated himself at the pilot's chair at the helm. "What the hell are ya thinking? What do ya think is on the other side? And if we do break through, who knows what could happen... I mean, what if there's a huge ocean of nasty stuff on the other side, and, I mean, hell, the puncture we make lets it all pour into our universe, drowns our universe in some foul substance..."

Richler, ignoring Kardov's speculations, says, "Ready the rockets. I'm backing us off a bit so the force of the explosions will have minimal effect. Okay, ready. Fire," and Kardov while still thinking it insane, follows through, pushing the launch triggers, since all of his training and success as a cosmonaut has taught him one thing — you always follow orders from a superior officer the likes of Commander James Richler.

Within seconds they witness large flower-like blasts bloom like large mushrooms, feel the slight repercussions from the explosions as if on an ocean and their boat was being rocked by a renegade wave. The two men both gaze into their macroscopic displayers, waiting for the light and gases from the blasts to dissipate. Richler now steers the ship closer to the barrier, the huge rent in front of them, only visible in the ship's headlights, and reflected from the jagged edges around the puncture they had created.

"We're going through," says Richler — Kardov still intent upon his displayer and muttering. "But it's black, all blackness, nothing. I can't see a thing..." as Richler steers the ship into the crevice, going at minimum speed since he too could see no thing, nothing but blackness.

★

It was some time before they realized they were a distance now on the other side of the barrier. Using their long-range scanners, they probed the space in front of them, until Kardov spotted it — a tiny speck of light perhaps hundreds of millions of light years away.

The two men were tense, fearful but excited as well. *So this is what it's like to be a true pioneer,* thought Kardov, following out loud with, "I've spotted something, but far too distant from us to even make an educated guess as to what it is. What do ya wanna do?"

Richler looking up from his scanner, saying simply "Continue," and then, "and let's get another beer."

"Ah hell, okay, I'll get us the special stuff, but com me if anything happens."

And with that Kardov leaves Richler alone, alone watching his scanners, alone with his thoughts about the unknown.

Back in the living quarters, as he's filling two steins with the special stock of red ale not generally available throughout the ship, Kardov thinks, *We couldn't have gone home anyway —*

too far, and it would've take too long — already took us fifty years to get to the barrier, and anyway, if the thing hadn't been there, we probably would've kept going until we died, and just kept sending back reports about nothing, reports they'd never respond to, probably thinking why waste the time, why waste our time responding to nothing with really nothing.

Kardov moves to a dry storage compartment, picks out some dehydrated pretzels, throws them into a bowl, pours water over them, and watches as they grow back to what they had been. *So now what? Continue where — to that distant dim glimmer definitely beyond what's left of our lifespan to reach, to discover, find out what the hell it is, what the hell is it? And what the hell was the barrier?*

The com suddenly blares to life. "Kardov, you better get up here, and bring the beer — I think we'll need it."

When Kardov enters forward command, Richler's voice is tense, edgy — "I didn't see it at first. The scanner picked it up five minutes ago. Something's coming towards us. You better sit down and have a good gulp of that beer, because if I'm right, it's a ship of some sort and it seems to be coming from that distant glimmer of light we saw previously."

Kardov rushes to his scanner, reads the display. "I can't really see it," he says.

"But you can see the heat signature the object is emitting," replies Richler.

Sure enough, Kardov knows that type of heat signature, the type emitted by some kind of vessel using a nuclear propulsion drive. "What do we do?"

"We wait," says Richler.

It is two days before they can actually see it. Its design is nothing like they've seen, and anyway it isn't from their home universe, on the other side of the barrier from which they've come. So they wait, and grow edgy — there isn't even an attempt to contact them through any kind of interstellar com system — and it will be some time before the alien craft reaches them.

"I don't understand this, I don't understand where we are or how this is happening." Kardov is feeling unpleasantly frightened, more than frightened. It seems everything he has believed in, been taught, has perceived, experienced and thought about the universe is crumbling in his mind into a mush of incoherence.

While they wait for the vessel to reach them — "Listen," Richler turns to Kardov who is chewing on pretzels while he tensely and alternatively switches his gaze between his camera display and scanner screens — "We don't know who these people are."

"Hell," Kardov interjects "they probably aren't people at all, aren't even human."

"Yes, that's probably true, but I've been thinking — they are probably or most definitely sentient beings…" Richler pauses, "and they'll have language. So I think while they're still traveling towards us, we better prepare the translator."

"We'll see if the bunch of junk works," Kardov says through a mouthful of pretzels.

The translator — provided by the Terra Interstellar Authority — is a supercomputer with a fifty terabyte program capable of translating any known or unknown language instantaneously, and the fact that it was built as an android with synthetic speech box will come in handy when they finally meet their alien newcomers.

"I'll be down in storage," says Richler, taking a swig from his stein before departing. "I'll get it up and running, " and quickly leaves.

★

They come.

They come towards them, come up close, manoeuvering their ship slowly, aligning their boarding dock with the two earthmen's ship.

When the air lock opens, Richler and Kardov can only stare. Two beings come slowly forward. They are at least two feet higher than both the terrans, and their skin is the deep hue of plums, their irises yellow on a black background. Otherwise they are perfectly humanoid in appearance.

The two groups stand facing one another, evaluating each other's appearance; the android translator standing to Richler's right.

"They'll have to speak first," Richler whispers to Kardov, and at that moment one of the visitors raises a hand and begins intoning in an unknown language, the android translator instantaneously reiterating what the visitor is saying, but in English. "Who are you? And what are you doing so far out here? We do not recognize your race. Where did you come from?"

Kardov slowly raises an arm and points back in the direction from which they have come, back in the direction of the barrier.

Both visitors suddenly look at each other. "Then we are saved," the same visitor states.

"What do you mean, saved?" Richler uneasily asks.

"You have come through that barrier that we have just discovered and have been exploring. Somehow you have come through, which means there is another universe on the other side, another universe our peoples can move to," continues the visitor.

This time Richler and Kardov look at each other.

"You see," the android translator continuing to translate the visitor's voice into English, "our universe was born in a tremendous burst, throwing itself outward in all directions. Just now the leading edge of our universe is speeding towards this place, and will reach that barrier, and will destroy itself when it reaches it, so we must evacuate as many of our peoples as possible to your universe on the other side."

Richler and Kardov can only stare, feeling nothing, as Kardov says, "Do you know what ale is? Would you like to try one?"

Sitting in a very large, very soft leather chair, Rhetor watches the flames dance. Occasionally he takes a sip from his glass, tasting the synthoholic liquid, lightly flavoured with cardamom and anise. For the moment, he is relaxed, musing on the patterns displayed in the holographic fireplace where the wood crackles, the flames leap, but emit no heat. He sits within a cavernous room divided into discrete spaces for relaxing, eating and sleeping, and the walls of which are lined with volumes of bound texts sitting upon floor-to-ceiling shelves, texts that were initially brought to him, and which he always is meant to declaim. For he is the Avatar of the Wording, each week speaking a new text to the customers, the populace of the place known as Arcopolis.

Rhetor's ears become alert as a door opens to his far right behind him, and he hears footsteps approaching as they resonate from the plastifloor.

"It will be within the hour," says Hilden, who has been Rhetor's aide-de-camp for as long as he can remember. Standing slightly in front of him, Hilden bows, saying, "The customers are being assembled throughout the net, and…"

"You know, Hilden," Rhetor interrupts, "I've been sitting here watching the flames dance in the hearth, my mind not being engaged, when I suddenly realized that I had forgotten something."

"Sir?" his aide respectfully inquires.

"Well, for instance, I couldn't remember the last Wording… and it was I who intoned it," says the Avatar, Hilden remaining silent. "So I retrieved the volume from the shelf over there and read the text, but…" Here Rhetor breaks off, a chill sensation suddenly traveling the length of his spine.

"My Avatar," Hilden speaks softly, "the commerce of language passes from you to the customers. Words are spent by you, never to return to you, since they now belong to others. The people own your words — you no longer have any need of them."

"I know… it's not that," and turning his gaze towards his aide who is now staring at his master, "Hilden, did I ever have a childhood?"

★

Scrambling through a mound of debris, his eyes intent on finding a treasure — any treasure — he fails to notice the ground shaking. As his hand reaches down to pick up a silvery object, the immense drainage pipe to his right erupts in a gush of garbage. Large and small objects, broken or simply discarded, made of metal or glass or flesh, fly at him. The violence of the impact of so much material throws him twenty feet from where he had been crouching, into another mound of debris, which begins to collapse over him.

"Foolish boy, foolish boy," he hears as if from afar — he coming to consciousness, darkness surrounding him. Not able to move, he listens. "I've told ya, haven't I, not ta git near tha gushers… ya just don' listen, do ya."

Hands touch him, grasp on to him, tug him forward. His eyes are suddenly full of light, but everything around him is blurry — his eyes being full of grit and tears.

"Look at cha," says the voice, a female voice. "I'm gonna hafta mend ya now. What a bother. It'll be days, days before…" The voice stops, cracked by emotion.

He feels himself lifted gently, carried in two arms, before he loses consciousness.

★

Rhetor's body shifts. His eyes slowly open, the room around him coming into focus in the dim glow of wall lights — for it is still night. Sitting up in bed, he rubs his eyes. The shelves of tomes tower around him in the semi-darkness, and he shivers, vaguely remembering a voice — someone's voice — "I'm gonna hafta mend ya now."

A familiar face wavers in his inner eye, then evaporates, leaving him staring at his slippers by the edge of his bed.

A sudden deflation of his inner strength suddenly overcomes him. He edges gingerly from his bed on to the plasti-floor, ignoring his slippers, and walks, as if in a trance, towards his very large, very soft leather chair.

He eases himself into his seat, and automatically his hand finds the remote, on the side table, with which he activates the holographic fireplace, but... the wood doesn't crackle, the flames don't leap... and his ears do not hear, his eyes do not see — he has fallen asleep.

★

"Oh, ya little man," he hears, and turns his head to the source of the voice. "My little man, what'm I gonna do wit' ya? Ha."

Some thing moves beside him. A dark, blurry form stoops over him.

"Here now, don'tcha move, I'm gonna wipe your eyes. Got a little water here."

A soft cloth — if that's what it is — moves across his closed eyelids, wiping away the grit, the encrustation, the tears, until he can see and look up. The stooping figure is in darkness, but he can make out its lower face, a mouth moving...

"There now... gotcha cleaned up... ha, but ya won't walk for a while," and the figure shuffles away from him, his eyes glimpsing a wax cylinder with its tip on fire, sitting on a... on a… *wooden table* — the two words, wooden and table, entering in his mind.

"Ya gotta mend quick, little man," she says "or we'll both be starvin'." The figure comes towards him, lowers itself, sits next to him — the dim light from the taper revealing a woman's face, a face weathered by time and concern. Hands move over him. They apply ointment. They begin to mend his broken parts.

"Where… ?" escapes his mouth in a breath.

★

"And so, lastly, while we may be surrounded by a world's misfortune beyond our control, we are secure in our customs and our homes. We can take solace — nay, joy! — Arcopolis sustains us as we sustain Her. The Wastes are beyond us, ever-threatening, but we can take comfort from our own selves. For have not we built Her with our own hands, with our own determination, to tower above the rubble? Therefore, I say to you, the customers of Arcopolis, let us continue to prosper, to work for Her, and She, in return, will reward us, will enrich us and secure our future." With these words, Rhetor closes the tome of the Wording, his vision looking out, beyond the balcony where he stands, upon the space where the screen is suspended in air, a screen with a billion pixels — the faces of the customers of Arcopolis.

Rhetor moves indoors, walks to a shelf where he places the tome of Wording never to be read from again. His mind is strangely blank, as if he were in a dreamless sleep.

The door to his room opens. Hilden approaches and stops before him.

"It is so," intones Hilden, "the Wording is accomplished, and Arcopolis will live again another day."

"Hilden… I know what you say and what it means, but… what did I speak to the customers? I don't remember."

"It is the Custom."

"Yes, yes," Rhetor interrupts impatiently, "but don't you find it strange that I can't remember what I said a few moments ago out on the balcony? After all, I remember what *you* have said to me in the past."

Hilden remains silent, his head bowed.

"And something else…" Rhetor continues, pausing briefly, "How did I get here?"

"My Avatar?" Hilden impassively looks into Rhetor's eyes.

"How did I come to be in this room? I seem to have lived my entire life here in this place. Is that so? All I can remember is this room, and you bringing my meals and comforts, bringing me a new tome of the Wording. Yet… I have dreams… of perhaps another life… when I was younger…"

"My Avatar, I cannot speak to this now. You are upset. But you need your rest, since you are spent from the Wording. I will speak with the Council to see if I may enlighten you, but for the nonce, please take your ease." Hilden bows gently. "I have brought you more of your favourite liquid refreshment. Rest your mind now, and when I return, hopefully we can speak of this matter further."

Rhetor watches Hilden leave, before moving to the side table where the newly arrived carafe of synthohol sits. He pours a glassful, then slumps into his armchair. *Hilden,* he thinks with affection, *has always taken care of me.*

★

"Mmm… tastes like pork, donnit? Ha, what'm I talkin' about — ya donno what pork is, do ya? Pigs — gone a long time ago, don't 'xist no more."

The boy watches the woman strip meat with her teeth from the bone. "What is it?" he asks.

"Found it near ya. Came from that gusher knocked you over. Could see it wasn't rotten, could make a good meal, feed us til you're up and about 'n' ready to scavenge for us." The woman eats as she talks. "Eat up now. Ya need your stength… mmm, roasted it for us right well I did."

The boy begins to eat. The flesh is slightly tough and stringy and seared in places, but delicious. His mind wanders. He thinks of his scavenging, the endless days of searching for food, water, utensils to make life slightly more bearable. Like yesterday when he found — what was it she called that? — a "potato peeler"?

"Come in handy if we find some vegables," she had said, when he handed it to her, not knowing what she was talking about.

"Vegables?" he asks.

"Nay, I'm pronouncin' it wrong — 'tis ve-ge-ta-bles. Say it."

"Ve-ge-ta-bles," he pronounces.

"'Sright, they use to grow all round from the ground. Good for eatin'. Don't see 'em any more though, so whatcha found might be useless."

After their meal, when she has retired for her noonday nap, he ambles outside of the makeshift abode within which they live. He notices something that hadn't been there before. It's green, about a foot tall, with what seem to be limbs, and is growing out of a barren patch of earth. It has small red globules growing on it. As he kneels beside it, his hand slowly touching the soft green thing, he whispers, "Ve-ge-ta-bles."

★

When Rhetor wakes, he sees Hilden seated across from him.

"Another dream?" asks his aide-de-camp. "You were talking in your sleep — something about vegetables."

"Yes," Rhetor replies.

"I have spoken with the Council," states Hilden with a slight tremor in his voice, "and while it may be dangerous, they felt it important, at this time, to relay to you the information you request. It was felt necessary, given your present mental state and, it seems, your increasing anxiety about your self."

"How so — dangerous?"

"My Avatar, you weren't always here, in this room. You were... found."

"Found?" inquires Rhetor.

"It has been a mere decade since... You see, Arcopolis has grown in the last ten years to become what it is today. Before then, it was a small impoverished village — a few huts, few people — trying to survive the Catastrophe. Plague and drought, and the overall decline of our planet's biosphere, led to disaster for humankind as well as to all other living organisms. I will not detail the present situation, except to say that very little can live outside of the Arcopolis. Briefly, my Avatar, to the north is the Iceland where no man ventures for fear of becoming a lifeless crystalline thing within minutes. To the west is the Devil's Anvil, a stark desert so furious that in its madness it can set a being on fire. To the east is the Bog, a lifeless ocean of bubbling mud where it is said unwholesome creatures abound. And to the south... is the Pit of Refuse, the destination of a system of drains through which, even in the days before the Arcopolis, we poured that which was broken or useless, decayed or spent, and where we flush our dead... it is there that we discovered you, my Avatar." Hilden becomes silent.

Rhetor doesn't speak.

"In those days," continues Hilden, "we would search that area, which was no more than the rubble of a past city. We would search for survivors and, as it came to pass, we found you. You were near death and, as we became aware, suffering coma. You were a boy of perhaps twelve years of age. We found you in a makeshift structure. Near where you lay on a cot, there was the desiccated corpse of what we identified as an elderly female. We took you from there. Our physicians tended to you for months. When you awoke from your coma, it was obvious to us that all your prior memories had been erased or, as is apparent now, suppressed, since your present dreams are…"

"Memories," Rhetor concludes. Staring at his aide-de-camp, he blurts, "But how is this possible? You say Arcopolis, a sprawling city of a billion customers, is a mere decade old. How could this be? From a few huts, as you said, to this… this…"

Hilden's face has become ashen. "My Avatar, there is something… we can't explain… but has become manifest since you were brought amongst us. When we found you… all about… outside the makeshift abode in which you were discovered… there were… *plants growing…*"

"Vegetables," replies Rhetor.

"Yes," exhales Hilden, "amidst other growth. My Avatar, there is more to tell but… I fear you need rest. I can sense your anxiety. You have many questions. Before we go on, however, you need to absorb what I have told you so far. I am your aide-de-camp, but I am also your friend, and, because of my affection for you…"

"What you have told me… I don't fully understand… and I fear what it bodes for me."

"It bodes well for you… and all of us… if you would just rest for now. We will continue later."

When Hilden has gone, Rhetor feels a great weariness despite his anxiety, and knows that he must sleep, must dream, but his sleep is short as is his dream.

★

"What's this then?" The old woman has come outside and is hovering over the young boy. "Found somethin', have ya?"

"Vegetable," says the boy.

"Whatcha talkin' bout? Haven't been any vegables for decades. Let me see." The old woman gently moves the boy aside to get a better look. "Whhhaaaaaa... . Geeeeees... . Ooonnuuuu." Wails erupt from her as her eyes encounter the plant. "Howww..." is her last word as she staggers backwards, her hand clutching her breast.

The boy scrambles to her side, looks into her open yet unseeing eyes.

★

When Rhetor wakens, tears are streaming down his face A throb in his chest propels him into violent sobbing, amidst which his anxiety begins to spiral up from within him. "Hilden! Hilden!" he cries out.

"My..." His words cut short as he sees his master's distress, Hilden rushes from the door, takes Rhetor's hands within his own. Forgetting his customary address, he tries to soothe with his voice. "Shhhh, now, shhhh, my friend, I'm here. It was just a memory... gone now. Shhhh, it'll be okay."

"Hilden, she dropped dead when... she saw the plant, the vegetable. Why?"

His aide-de-camp, still clasping hands, replies, "Because the plant wasn't supposed to be there... because you made it be there."

Rhetor uncomprehendingly looks to his friend.

"I must tell you now," Hilden begins. "Do you know why you are the Avatar of the Wording?"

Rhetor shakes his head.

"It's because you're special, different from other men — you have a gift." Hilden continues. "We don't know how or why but... when you speak... as the Avatar, it as if you're in a dream. You lose all consciousness of yourself, and what you speak — the Wording, as it has become our custom to call it since you came among us — it makes the world become... as if reality itself was born from your mouth..."

Rhetor flares up. "What nonsense! Why are you speaking such rubbish! Do you expect me to believe I'm... I'm... No, you're wrong... the vegetable, plant, whatever — it just grew there. I didn't wish it into being."

Hilden looks at him intently. "You built Arcopolis."

"More nonsense. Our people built it."

"But the Wording..." replies Hilden.

"Granted, I can never remember what I speak when addressing the customers. The words don't seem to mean anything to me, so having no import, why should I remember them? If it as you say, this nonsense you talk, then should I stop the Wording — you would have me believe the Arcopolis would not evolve, or worse, would cease to be?"

Having said that, Rhetor sees that Hilden has gone pale. His eyes are bulging and there is a look of sheer terror on his face.

Softly Rhetor says, "This is nonsense, my friend. I can show you. Tomorrow I will not perform the Wording. You will see. We will all be here the day after."

"Nooo!" Hilden yells and rushes from the room.

Shocked by Hilden's sudden departure, Rhetor feels uncertain. A shiver runs up his spine. "So if I said... if I said..." but he stops himself, as an unknown dread creeps over him. He thinks, *It can't be...*

★

No dreams. No more dreams. After she died, what happened? Why don't I remember? Rhetor arises from his bed, dresses slowly.

The door to his room opens. Hilden approaches in a posture of supplication.

"My Avatar, may I speak with you."

Rhetor remains silent.

"The Council has advised that I talk with you, as I am your familiar, and have been since your arrival here. Whatever you think of what I have told you, of your gift, of your past, I implore you to believe me, albeit my talk yesterday may strike you as fantastic and improbable. If only for our friendship, trust me. Perform the Wording, even though the words are not your own and they have no import for you."

Rhetor paces uneasily. "Have I been outside these walls, Hilden? Have I walked through Arcopolis, seen its people, its evolution?"

"Yes, many times, and in my company."

"Then why can't I remember?" snaps Rhetor.

"We do not know, my Avatar. Some suspect your present condition may have been due to past trauma related to your coma."

"I don't know either," but instantly Rhetor remembers the old woman falling over, ceasing to live, when he said the word *vegetable*. Did he kill her... with a word?

"My Avatar, I know that you are confused, and incredulous at what I have told you. You said yesterday that you would not perform the Wording today. I informed the Council of your stated decision. They have given me something to give you. It is an artifact, a book, one of the few remaining in this world, one of the few we could salvage from the ruins of our past civilization, before the Arcopolis. The Council has asked that you read it before you make any decision. While all it purports may not be true, I trust it will have some meaning for you. I will place it here and leave you in peace. Call me if you have a need."

Hilden having left, Rhetor allows himself a brief spasm of a sob. *How dear is Hilden. Why am I so confused? Can I deny his request?* he thinks. Slowly he moves to the dining table where

Hilden has left the book. He eases himself into a chair, takes the book within his hands — a hard-bound book, with words inscribed on its cover that he doesn't understand. He forgets everything else, overcome with curiosity. He opens the tome, finds what he perceives to be the initial passage and begins reading:

"In the Beginning was the Word…"

UNEXPECTED PASSAGE

Gaddis looked out from the dining room in the stern of the Princess Carla, and watched the receding skyline of Manhattan across New York Harbour. He had lucked out and gotten a window seat, so he could sip his morning coffee and watch the beginning of his maiden voyage. His thoughts wandered aimlessly, from the concert he had attended yesterday to considerations for his earned sojourn. What would he do once he reached Puerto Rico? He could've taken a plane, faster of course, but thought that a true voyage had to be by boat.

"Will you be having breakfast, Mr. Gaddis?" asked the waiter who had suddenly materialized beside his table.

"Please, yes. I'll have two eggs, over easy, with sausages and hash browns, and no toast. Oh, and I'd like some more coffee, thanks."

The waiter retired to get his order, as Gaddis returned his attention to the vista beyond the ship, and thought of the band he had seen last night. *The Music Machine — another one-hit wonder*, he mused, *but a solid performance, nonetheless.*

He breathed a sigh. *Puerto Rico, here I come*, but also knew that it wouldn't be all rest and relaxation. He had his book to finish, and had taken his sabbatical at this time to insure he did. A good spell away from his professorship of History at NYU was just what he needed.

★

After breakfast, Gaddis strolled out and found the lee side of the cruise liner, where he stood leisurely smoking a cigarette. His eyes took in the ocean vista, the green-blue waves rolling all around the ship, and thought of his book's thesis. His study of all the ancient Grecian texts, from histories to poetry, had led to an inevitable conclusion. Human visual perception had made a startling jump in evolution. In all early texts, the colour of the seas was designated as *red*, and it was only in later texts that there arose mention of the seas as being *green* or *blue*, in the opposite spectrum. How had this come about, and why?

Gaddis suddenly felt another's presence, and turned his gaze to the right.

"Hey, man, how ya doin'," said an Asian-looking young man with shoulder-length straight black hair, dressed in a sweatshirt and jeans, a silver stud in his right ear, and coloured beads around his neck.

"The name's George… George Sands. Takin' a voyage too, eh? Ain't it cool?"

"Yes, it's wonderful," replied Gaddis, feeling at ease with this type of person, since he had many of his ilk, both male and female, in his classes back at NYU.

"Hey, ya know somethin'? The route we're on to Puerto Rico, ya know, well… get this — it takes us through an edge of the Bermuda Triangle. Ya heard of it? Like, planes and ships seem to just disappear there. Like, wow man, hope that doesn't happen to us!"

Gaddis noticed the lit rolled cigarette in the young man's right hand.

"Oh, sorry man, you wanna toke?" asked George politely.

"No thanks," replied Gaddis, "I'm a scotch-and-soda man myself."

"Ya, that's cool," and George turned his attention out to sea. "Like, look at that colour, man!"

★

That evening, after dining on oysters-on-the-half-shell with escargots, and consuming a half-litre of Chianti, Gaddis retired to his cabin in a mellow emotional glow. Thinking of his meeting that afternoon with Mr. Sands, *I wonder if he writes poetry*, he mused.

As a young man, Gaddis himself had penned poetry, but later had found his inspiration through literary fiction. His intellectual and professional pursuits, of course, were devoted to History and Philosophy, but fiction was a realm for his imagination where he could explore the metaphors of reality and existence. After all, Jules Verne had imagined the submarine long before that vessel came into reality; and the term 'fiction' was a misnomer as far as Gaddis was concerned.

Imagination, for Gaddis, was like having a structured dream life, yet in full consciousness and able to be directed. *Dreams, after all*, thought Gaddis, *are messengers of our imagination*, and with that in his mind, he climbed into bed and was abruptly in a deep sleep.

Hey man, like, you ever read Lord of the Flies? *Gaddis stared at George Sands, whose face had taken on Negroid features, and whose skin was dark brown. It's about cannabalism, man... about survival of the fittest. Gaddis found he couldn't talk, his mouth wouldn't move. Ya think that happened in the Bermuda Triangle, man? Gaddis saw that Sands was striking together two stones over a heap of kindling. Fire, man, we need fire... can't eat shit raw, man!*

Gaddis woke up to find himself in a hot sweat. *Messengers of our imagination indeed*, he wondered.

★

Over the course of the voyage, Gaddis happened to meet Sands again. Having dismissed his dream as the result of too much Chianti and an over-active imagination, he approached Sands one day on deck.

After a nod of recognition between them, Gaddis said, "By the way, all those stories you've perhaps heard about the Bermuda Triangle... there's a perfectly rational explanation for those ships that disappeared. The culprit is methane hydrate that's emitted by undersea mud volcanoes. It creates a type of frothy water that becomes incapable of providing adequate buoyancy for ships, so that the area around a ship can cause a vessel to sink very rapidly and without warning."

"But the planes, man… what about the planes that disappeared. Does this frothy water suck them out of the sky?" Sands replied with an impish smile, "But hey man, we'll find out soon enough. One of the crew just told me we're about an hour away from entering the Bermuda Triangle."

Gaddis found himself at a loss for words, and turned to stare out at the sea, whilst lighting a cigarette.

★

His book was to be titled *Invisible Horizons*, with the sub-title *a study of the edges of perception*; and he felt that, somehow, mankind's eagerness to explore and expand his horizon was basic to his visual evolution, so that the sea could turn from red to blue. But what perplexed Gaddis was the timeline. This shift in perception happened over only two millennia, and he knew, from his reading of Darwin, that evolution happens much more slowly, in fact — over millions of years. So why was the evolutionary process sped up in this instance? Was there more at stake back then that the Greek historians and poets weren't telling us — perhaps this abnormal acceleration in visual acuity was brought on by the unconscious awareness of a threat to the survival of our species? But what was the threat?

Gaddis was musing over this at the desk in his cabin, when there was a knock at the door. Opening it, he was confronted with an eager, smiling Mr. Sands.

"Hey man, we're there!"

Gaddis replied, "Well, I'm working right now, but you be sure to come and tell me if we disappear."

"Oh man, no need to be rude," still smiling, Sands said. "This is, like, a historic moment for me. Maybe you want to join me, and have a smoke, man."

Gaddis smiled to himself, and thought, *Okay, I can work when I get to Puerto Rico*, and replied, "Sure, a break will do me good," and proceeded on to the deck with his new companion.

Nothing, of course, was happening. The sea here in the Triangle looked just like the sea outside it, but Sands now was intently staring at and watching the water around the ship.

Feeling somewhat sorry for the boy, Gaddis turned to him.

"Sands, would you like to have dinner with me tonight?"

"Sure, man, that sounds great. What time?"

"Let's say seven. I've got a nice window table reserved," and the two parted company, with Sands waving to him, as if Gaddis was his new best friend.

★

"Oh man, there's nothing but fish and meat here. I'm a vegetarian, man, don't eat animals of any kind," complained Sands.

"Actually," and Gaddis pointed to the menu, "the pasta Alfredo is very good, and I'm sure they would substitute the vegetable of your choice for the chicken."

"Okay man, that sounds good."

"Can I pour you some Chianti?" Gaddis asked.

"No man, I'm okay with water... but do ya think they might have juice or herbal tea?"

"Why don't you ask?" replied Gaddis.

They both sat for some time in silence, staring out at the blackness of night, at the ocean that would momentarily glint the moonlight off its swells. Even when dinner was served and they had been eating for some time, they both remained unspeaking. It was only towards the end of the meal that things began to happen.

"Holy shit, man! Did you feel that?!" Sands nearly shouted.

"What?" asked Gaddis, a little stupefied.

"It's like in a plane, man. Didn't you feel us drop? We dropped, man!"

Gaddis stared at Sands, but had to admit to himself that he too had felt it — a type of subtle centrifugal force directed vertically downward — a sensation he always primarily felt in his stomach. He suddenly had the urge to stand up, and did so. In that moment, the dinner table slid away from him towards Sands and knocked the young man out of his chair. He couldn't see Sands, but only hear his, "Fuck, man, did you do that?" Gaddis grasped the nearby window sash and looked around. The other diners were swiftly exiting the room, the waiters were nowhere to be seen, and the ship's intercom blared to life.

"Attention passengers, please move to the main deck and locate the nearest lifeboat station. Members of the crew will assist you in debarkation."

There was no mention of what was happening.

My research and papers, Gaddis thought, and ran to his cabin, leaving Sands behind to fend for himself. Reaching his room, he gathered together everything of importance and stuffed it in his valise, but in the blink of an eye he felt a change. The ship seemed strangely still and silent. He looked up at the portal in his cabin, and his mind refused to believe what his eyes saw.

"But it's night," he said aloud, as he perceived sunlight streaming through the portal.

★

Slowly and cautiously, Gaddis made his way through the ship's inner corridors, and finally stepped out on to the main deck. There was not a soul in sight, and apparently, as he looked further, all the lifeboats were gone. The sun was shining directly overhead, and the ship didn't seemed to be moving, or more correctly, to be powered, but was simply floating along on some unseen current. He looked out at the sea, and stood puzzled. There were no waves, no tides… the ocean's surface was like a flat mirror, and looking down over the ship's railing, he felt vertiginously faint because he was staring down into the sky, which was simply reflected back at him in perfect imagery.

Shaken, Gaddis found a deck chair and sat down. Lighting a cigarette, he began to think as coherently as he could; after all, he was a philosophic person, and had never allowed himself to be victimized by raw emotion. As he sat, he noticed there was no wind, not even the subtle waft of a breeze. A slightly hysterical chuckle arose in him as he remembered the river Styx, the boatman Charon… *but I can't be dead*, he thought. Pinching himself, he watched a small area of skin on his left forearm turn momentarily red. *Ergo cogito sum?* he queried himself, and then stood up.

While he could have continued to sit, and philosophize, his body was too upset. He *had* to move, and, in moving, he sensed that the seeming physical reality around him would be best met and understood by his own physical being. *But where to go, and where to start… and what do I do?* he asked himself.

He made his way to the prow of the ship, taking with him one of the numerous deck chairs and, upon arriving, plunked it down, where he sat and could have a full view of the horizon before him, a horizon of no detail, a horizon towards which the ship seemed to be floating. He drew and lit another cigarette, his mind empty but for the vista in front of him, his body then succumbing to stress caused by this phenomenal situation. He nodded off.

★

"Holy fuck, man!"

Gaddis thought he was dreaming... *Go away, go away...* the memory of his previous dream that had included Sands coming back to him.

"Why d'ya go away, man?"

Gaddis was suddenly alert, and looked behind him from his seat on the prow. George Sands was limping towards him, a look on his face more of misery and confusion than of anger. Gaddis stood up.

"George, are you okay?" and as he said this, Gaddis felt relief sweep over him, and an empathy that had been absent in his previous dealings with Sands.

"No, man, look at my leg. After you left, I slid around on my back in that dining room, and crashed into things until it stopped. What's happening?"

"Here," and Gaddis motioned to the deck chair, "Sit down... let me have a look at that leg."

Sands complied.

"Your leg will be okay, just badly bruised, and George... I don't know what's *happening*," Gaddis stressing his last word for the benefit of his hearer.

"Where are we?" Sands asked while his eyes took in the empty, seemingly endless horizon.

"I don't know," replied Gaddis. "Perhaps we're inside the Bermuda Triangle?" and he suddenly felt at a loss to impart anything resembling knowledge or wisdom to the young man, and could see that his companion was terrified, and so became silent.

★

Towards evening, Gaddis saw that Sands was moving about, hardly limping, and, amazingly, taking the situation in a reasonable way.

"Hey man, what's your first name?"

"Vincent," replied Gaddis.

"It's okay then… that I call you Vince… don't hafta say *man* all the time?"

"Sure."

"Hey Vince, I don't know what the fuck is happening… but I feel, like, it's the best vacation I've been on in years. In fact, if this is a 'nother reality, I don't have to follow through on my contract. None of your business… but shit, given this, won't hurt to tell ya. I'm a mule. Know what that is?"

"Yes," replied Gaddis.

Sands stared at Gaddis with a quizzical look.

"So, like, you're okay with it?"

"Not my concern, and besides, peddling dope isn't going to get us anywhere, " said Gaddis. "Perhaps you haven't noticed… there's no wind, not even a breeze; there's no waves on the water which is as still and flat as glass; and there're no locomotion on this ship… it just seems to be floating in a current… a current that's going that way," and Gaddis pointed straight towards the ship's prow.

Sands continued to stare at Gaddis.

"George, this isn't *Lord of the Flies*, and I won't eat you. We've got enough types of food on this ship to last us for months. But my guess is we'll see some land at some point, probably sooner than later… I don't think…" but Gaddis stopped himself, continuing to speculate, and not able to accept anything else than a rational, albeit perhaps 'imaginatively' rational answer to their phenomenal predicament.

"Why don't I make us a great salad?" asked Gaddis, "You must be hungry. How about mixed greens, some unripe olives, sliced tomatoes and sweet white onions, chick peas, cucumber, and a sprinkle of dill seed… with a blue-cheese dressing?"

"Okay, Vince. Whatya mean by 'unripe'?"

So, that evening, George and Vince dined, having a simple but delectable meatless meal; and Sands, for the first time in his life, imbibed alcohol, sipping one of the ship pantry's most exquisite Burgundy wines.

★

The next morning both men were on the deck's prow, both standing with a cup of coffee in one hand and their preferred smokes in the other.

"Hey, Vince, why does the water look red?"

Gaddis was lost in thought, and didn't hear his companion.

Both looked out and now saw what they could only presume to be land. As they grew closer, what at first, to their eyes, looked like a thin strip of ground, grew until their peripheral vision recognized that this was no mere atoll or desert isle. The shores receded at right angles almost infinitely. They seemed headed towards a thin strip of beach, and the perceivable flora that edged it looked strangely familiar and alien at the same time, nothing like one would expect to see in the Caribbean.

The large ocean liner finally crunched itself on a coastal shoal, both Gaddis and Sands being thrown off balance and falling to the deck.

"Hey, Vince," Sands called out.

"Time to go ashore, I think, George… we can always come back for food and drink. Let's find out where we are, if anywhere," and for the first time in his life, Gaddis allowed another voice inside his self to say *Fuck me!*

The two men then negotiated the metal ladder over the side of the boat, and swam the hundred or so yards to the shore. As they reached the beach, wet and panting, something stirred in front of them, and before they could either stand or perceive its detail, they were surrounded by what looked like military personnel in full combat array, and who held weapons that were pointed directly at them.

"Welcome gentlemen," Gaddis heard and, looking up, perceived a person approaching in what he recognized as USA service dress khaki, a style in vogue in the Pacific arena of the Second World War.

"Where are we?" Gaddis asked, kneeling on the sand.

"You'll be well taken care of," began the man. "Just don't expect to attack our nation again!" he then shouted.

Sands began to whimper, then suddenly ran off screaming. He was shot down instantly.

Gaddis, thoroughly shaken but now angry, asked, "Where am I?"

The man in khaki, who seemed to be the spokesman, replied, "Right here, where you're supposed to be, you fuckin' Jap sympathizer."

BERLIN ABSTRACT

What universal hatred! What unmitigated revulsion towards *me*! They called me a "cannibal"! Why? When all I ever wanted was to help, was to see our nation strong and unthreatened by those barbarian cultures at our borders who wished us weakened, why should I and others of my countrymen end up so? For posterity then, and to show how our race can rise above adversity, I shall write this abstract of my present thoughts.

History has recorded (albeit from those self-righteous victors' perspective) our physical, intellectual and spiritual evolution, which others sneeringly contradict and term 'devolution.' The details of the struggle to regain our nation, to regain our self-esteem after our embarrassing defeat in the first War, are unnecessary to repeat here. I was but an idealistic young man then, aspiring to be an artist, and when I learned of that coming conflict, I fell on my knees and thanked Providence, for I felt a heroic, noble destiny beginning to unfold before me. The history of the second War also is of no consequence, as it has been eclipsed by the passing of years.

Rather than dwell upon those times then, I wish to talk obliquely from History, talk of the dream, talk of those last months before I traveled to this place, this time in the twenty-first century. But first, think of this — if you, following the course of your existence, had found your purpose, a purpose that filled every moment of your waking life, filled you with a strength of self that allowed you to actualize all that you had dreamt, all you had hoped for — would you second-guess it, preferring instead some comfortable living, some boring nondescript occupation without challenge? This is what you must consider as you read this abstract.

★

The first indication of the possibility came in that last year when, despite our strength and reserve, our nation was buffeted on all sides by the barbarian hordes — the Francs, the Slavs, the Anglos, all wanted to effect our extermination and bring the great dream crashing into the hallowed ground we had built upon, the great dream we had nourished and grown beyond every boundary and barrier in order to bring a new world to life.

His name was Hans Fricker, and it was he who held the possibility. A relatively non-descript short individual he was, who wore clean but shabby clothes, and was balding despite his youthful age of thirty-five, but whose eyes burned with an intensity that hinted at a single-purposed person, and were constantly red-rimmed and darting this way and that. He had come at the request of my companion, Eva, and was to join us, along with an entourage of gentlemen and ladies of my acquaintance, at my chalet for an afternoon picnic. Eva had told me something of this little man, relating that he was possibly the greatest biologist and mechanical engineer in all the lands, but who had been rejected by his scientific colleagues as a crank, and not accepted by any of the distinguished scientific institutions that normally granted recognition and honours upon those of higher gifts.

I was standing near a railing of the large terrace we used in fair weather for parties and receptions, sipping tea, and chatting amiably with a well-known poet and his wife when I saw Eva enter with Fricker at her side. She took him directly to Martin, for no one has access to my personage without the discretion of my personal secretary. As I conversed with the poet on the subjects of imagination and metaphor, I kept watch on Fricker, who looked rather uncomfortable, having not expected such a lengthy interview with Martin. Finally their talk had come to an end and Eva, taking Fricker by the arm, guided the man towards me.

Stopping before me, and smiling genially albeit nervously, he gave his salutation, "My Leader, I am greatly pleased to meet you at last."

I thought a direct reply would be best, and one which would betray any emotion in him of a corrupt or unhealthy nature. "Are you a Jew?" I queried.

He smiled. "No, My Leader. I'm a biologist," and we both laughed.

"I have something that I feel would be of great importance to you and your future," he said, "but I fear to speak of it, being surrounded, as we are, by other ears."

I suddenly liked this man. He displayed a healthy paranoia, so I motioned that we should walk to the far end of the terrace which was deserted of persons, and which was furnished with comfortable chairs and tables under large parasols.

★

For some time I sat uncomprehendingly as words poured into my ears. I watched Fricker's mouth moving, as dimly I became aware of such words as 'a time to come' and 'begin the work again.'

Fricker said, "I understand it is going badly at present."

His comment insulted me, since this 'it,' the present world conflict with which I was engaged, was integral to my dream, my purpose, and my dreams and purposes are nothing other than myself incarnate — "Nothing is going badly!" I hissed at him, feeling violence arising within me.

"I meant no offense," replied Fricker, and he bowed his head momentarily before his eyes came up to meet mine, and with an odd look, both unfearful and conspiratorial, he continued, "but if it should happen that the Gods themselves wished to wipe the earth of the Jew, the homosexual or the communist, and in doing so inadvertently caused the extinction of numerous bystanders, would it not be good to have a contingency plan to safeguard your ambitions, so that they could be realized in a future time?"

I remained silent, trying to calm myself, realizing this was no ordinary creature come to insult me.

"Theory, if I may say so, My Leader, is not some whimsical thought, not some imagined solution. It is, quite simply, all our acquired and accumulated knowledge that exists about a thing. And if that knowledge happens to change, to evolve, we adapt our thinking to accommodate this new information. In the past whole systems of belief were overthrown in such a manner. But today, the scientific method allows us the wisdom of our mistakes, so our knowledge and our theories are secure in the present, and through a process of accretion, rather than subtraction, they grow rather than are diminished. No one today would challenge the theory of Gravity, for instance. It's an established fact with no further evidence to dispute it. Yet we call this fact — a theory," and he looked at me with emotionally inflamed eyes.

"Well?" I urged him to continue, now having settled in myself that I could begin to like this man.

"My Leader, consider the following. If a man, who had been thoroughly crushed in his war against infidels, could survive the vagaries of time, and live another day to continue his battle, with a greater wisdom in hindsight, and be victorious, see his dreams of a better world actualized, would not the cost of such a survival be worth paying?"

"What do you mean?" I asked him.

"My Leader, I am a biologist and a mechanical engineer. I have also made certain study into other areas of science, primarily one field of exploration yet in its infancy — genetics, and which I alone have managed to decrypt. My colleagues are mostly in the fog about it. No matter. I have conspired my disciplines together and, with the addition of this new science, have found a way to escape the present and live in the future!"

I looked at the man, thinking now that he must be some sort of alchemical dreamer or mad scientist, and stated, "You can't escape the present."

A twinkle lit his eyes, and he paused momentarily, and I could see him thinking deliberately of what to say next.

"My Leader, if it be your pleasure and interest, I would like to invite you to my laboratory facilities. I think it would be better if you were to see with your own eyes the reality of my research as I explain it. Otherwise, it would seem to you but an abstract idea."

Looking at Fricker, and thinking that perhaps this was another elaborate trap to assassinate me, I replied, "Let me think on it, and I shall contact you two days hence," and with that I arose, while Eva came to chat with the small man, and I walked toward the open terrace doors to my study, motioning to Martin to follow me.

"I would like you to gather information about this man. See what the SS knows. He's talking obscurely, won't tell me directly what it is he's up to. Rather, he wants me to visit his labs. We have to be very careful here. I don't want a repeat of that Stauffenberg affair."

"Yes, My Leader," said Martin and left me, as I mused about the present, and what the future possibly could hold.

★

Martin came to me two days later.

"I believe he is the real thing," he reported, "an authentic, uncommon mind, and from what I could understand and see for myself, he's created a new form of technology, a type of time-travel device."

"That's impossible!" I nearly shouted. "One can not travel in time, since time does not exist, Martin. There is only the present moment. Our minds have invented time as a convenience, and time only exists in our minds as memory and as the progression of existence. Do you actually believe this fool?"

"I don't believe he's a fool," replied Martin, "in fact, I think he's a genius. I can't explain it to you. You'll have to go there yourself, and see and hear about this amazing invention. My words and knowledge are insufficient to give you a full debriefing."

"Well, what do you propose?"

"My Leader, I have stationed a small elite corps of veteran soldiers at his site. His laboratories are hidden from the world, carved out beneath the Herzogenhorn mountain in the southern Black Forest. Fricker didn't mind, saying he understood the need for your security. In fact, though you just met the man, I believe he is devoted to you, as many of us are."

I thought a moment. "Fine. We'll go, but I want a special unit of some of our best SS to accompany us," and feeling somewhat spirited by this excursion I concluded, "let's see what Time has in store for us."

★

What a wonderous thing this is, I thought, as we traveled along the cavernous tunnels that had been expertly constructed beneath Herzogenhorn, the sweet smell of gasoline in the air as the convoy of staff cars progressed along the main thoroughfare that had a faint slope in its descent.

"Why were we not aware of this facility?" I asked Martin, turning to him seated beside me in the back of the sedan.

"Apparently, My Leader, Fricker was under instructions to keep it secret."

"Who gave those instructions, and without my assent," I snapped.

"It is my understanding, My Leader, as related to me by Fricker," replied Martin, "that this facility was financed by a group of very powerful and wealthy pan-national industrialists who, having learned of the scientist's experiments, indentured him. They are a Star Chamber of sorts. Having the same goal as your self, they too long for a New World Order, one in which our Fatherland is the pivot. But unlike your self, they believe the present time is not propitious, that this new American state, with its youthful albeit naïve ideologies, has military strength unseen in prior times, and will probably prevail in the present War. These men prefer not confrontation, not the waste of war, but a slow infiltration of all societies, using finance, commerce and technology to herd the people and render them pliant and complacent. However, they do see you as a leader, as a man of great gifts and oratory, so they sent Fricker on reconnaissance to you, in the hope you would join them at their side."

Martin then fell silent as our convoy entered the courtyard of an immense cavern. Surrounding the courtyard on all circumferential sides, but for the tunnel exit from which we had emerged, stood numerous buildings, some three and four stories high. Various figures clad in scientific and medical garb could be seen entering and exiting the various structures. Our motorcade proceeded to a central large complex at the far end of the courtyard. As our cars pulled up, Fricker emerged from the complex and strode towards us.

"Welcome, My Leader, it gives me the greatest of pleasure that you have decided to grace me with your presence," announced the little man.

Not wishing to encourage any surperfluous talk, I motioned to the complex of buildings from which Fricker had come, and began striding towards them with Martin at my side and the little man in hot pursuit.

★

Having taken the lead, Fricker led us through a maze of hallways, and finally to a very large room with double doors which he bade us enter.

At first, my eyes needed to adjust themselves, for the interior of this room was dimly lit. Along the circumferences were various workstations covered with beakers, microscopes and other scientific and medical paraphernalia, and lit by small overhead lamps that emitted a soft greenish light. I felt a slight astonishment, however, when I perceived the middle area of the space. Lined up, in neat rows, were a number of cylindrical tubes settled on biers. Measuring about four metres in length and two in diameter, they also were lit by a greenish light, but from the interior, for the tops of the tubes, which faced the ceiling, seemed made of a transparent material, perhaps glass. What had surprised me, though, was that there were people within the tubes.

Fricker, seeing my surprise, slowly sidled to my side. "It shortly will be their time to wake," he said in a soft voice. "They have been there for a number of years, since we completed this facility, my research having concluded a good decade ago."

"But what is this?" I queried.

"You see before you, My Leader, a sort of time machine, a portal to the future. It's called cryogenetics. I won't bore you with the scientific and medical details. Suffice it to say that a man can be placed in a state of suspended animation, a hibernation of sorts. His body is 'frozen,' so to speak. His bodily rhythms and functions are slowed to a miniscule level of operation, and he visibly does not age. He is, in effect, preserved, and can remain in that state for hundreds of years. Of course, his suspended state must be monitored occasionally, and he must be nourished intravenously. When the designated time has come, he is 'unfrozen' and can once again pursue life, while retaining the health and age he possessed before entering the procedure."

"I see," I said, a rush of thoughts and possibilities invading my mind.

"And I'm sure you see also, My Leader, the advantage to you and yours, and to our cause. While the New World Order may not come about today, there is always the future," and Fricker then fell silent.

I gazed at the bodies in the tubes. "Is there a plan?" I asked firmly.

"Yes, My Leader," answered the little man. "As Martin has no doubt told you, this enterprise is supported by a group of very rich and influential people, a Star Chamber, as it were, not focused upon judgement but upon the accumulation of wealth and power. They see the present conflict, and all wars in fact, as counterproductive, and believe there are other means and methods to gain mastery of the world. Their vision is to give the masses of humanity what they want, while at the same time enticing them to want more. In this way, the people are not unrestful, but become 'satisfied,' eagerly buying up all the technological gadgets, styles of clothing, means of transport, et alia that we can provide, at a cost of course."

"Commercial sovereignty."

"Yes, My Leader," said Fricker, "I knew you would grasp the matter and, perhaps now, you also can see its implications."

"And my place in this?" I asked.

"You will become an honoured member of the group — let's call it the Chamber of Commerce, the title they tentatively have given the collective."

★

And so, it came to pass that, upon opening my eyes, the first things I saw were the faces of Eva and Martin on my left, and that of Fricker on my right, all cast in a greenish glow.

"Welcome back," Fricker simply said.

I sit at my desk now, writing these words, in a high tower that rises majestically from the floor of the city. Occasionally I gaze down through the large plate-glass windows of my office, watching the activity on the streets of New York below, watching all the tiny creatures scurrying to and fro on foot or in vehicles.

It is an exciting time, this twenty-first century, a time of wealth and progress for our kind, for our race, for our group. Today is especially exciting, for the meeting of our Chamber will put into effect its master stroke like the lash of a whip.

The herds below, being fickle and obsessive, will buy it wholesale. Every new gadget, every new toy we have brought to the market, they have embraced unhesitatingly. The various communication and entertainment devices that we have provided, that they carry about with them daily, providing them with a distracting convenience, are now a necessity. Their compulsive and consuming need to talk constantly about themselves, to display themselves, to do their business every moment of the day, have replaced any moments of deeper contemplation. They are ripe! Even now, they complain about having to carry these devices about, how it inconveniences them, and we have listened as the herds' chorus has increased.

With our applied sciences, we will supply them with a new bionic future — every device becoming part of the body, wired directly to their nervous systems, to their brains. They will have what they want, and we, the Chamber, will have what we want. We'll just, as it were, flip the switch.

I shall be happy to bear all the responsibility, with my colleagues, for what is to come. The only thing I should not be able to bear would be weakness in the face of our endeavour.

The life that is ours should serve only one task — namely, to make up for all the wrongs done by the international mongrel races to our dreams. A good century ago, I predicted victory for my Fatherland. Today I sense that victory is finally ours. We shall have what we want, what we envisioned. We shall have a New World Order. We shall have our Fourth Reich.

LUNAR PENTATONICS

we investigate dust and observe death
make sex a silhouette
then sculpt our pain

Catherine Mead sat back in her chair, and read over the almost
epigrammatic poem she had just written, realizing that it had
fallen short, that, at this point in her life, she could be neither
witty nor clever. Yet the lines resonated with her. They somehow captured what she still felt commanded her nervous system, even though she went to great troubles to subvert her
behaviour, to act out of considered thought rather than spon-
taneous desire or passion. The emerging terror of an inevitabil-
ity, of an inescapable predestination, produced severe panic
attacks that immobilized her, and censored the imagination
which was her one true gift as a writer.

One such attack, however, had so frightened her that she
involuntarily acted as if in self-defense. It had led her here to
the Toronto Islands and the Gibraltar Point Centre for the Arts.
She saw her escape to this place, an escape from the neurotic
routines of her life, as offering both refuge and an antidote to
the inevitable silencing of her writing.

"Fuck," she said, and stood up from her chair in the space
that served as both studio and bed-sitting room. She looked
down at her laptop screen, then out the small window in front
of her, and thought out loud "sculpt our pain..." but before
she could continue with any other thought, her eyes caught
the figure of a line of cormorants rising from the tree line that
separated the Colony from the lake. *Perhaps it's time for a walk,*
she thought, and she proceeded to exit her room.

★

Magic moments in nature are only revealed to the observer when least expected and yet only when the onlooker is in a trance of observation. It was one such moment when Catherine, seated on a picnic table on the beach, found herself watching a single file of perhaps fourteen geese out paddling in the lake. That the birds' feet under water were moving swiftly was not apparent, so effortlessly they seemed to glide, and then in a moment the leader of this seeming convoy turned its head and honked a short three syllables, whereupon the second in line caught up the sound, and relayed it to the third in line, and the refrain continued on down to the last bird, and without any delay the leader lifted off from the water as the entire retinue followed in a graceful linear ascent.

Catherine sat in wonder, thinking about the nature of communication.

"That's a grand sight, isn't it?"

Turning her head, as if she were waking from a deep sleep, she perceived the source of this spoken appraisal. Here was a man, perhaps in his early fifties, no more than five feet in height, with a small yet well groomed moustache and goatee, and a bushy head of fiery red hair. A slight bit on the beefy side but not overweight, he wore a wide-brimmed black hat that Catherine surmised was leather. Yet despite it being a hot August and being on the beach, he was fully clothed with long-sleeved woolen shirt and denim jeans, and oddly a very large pair of heavy leather boots shod his feet.

"Hello," said Catherine.

"My, it's a fine evening for contemplation and communication, don't ya think?" said the man, and smiled warmly; but all Catherine could do was gaze at his eyes, which were gazing back at her, because the irises of his eyes were silver, such a light silver shade that they practically disappeared into the sclera.

"Oh, I'm sorry if I've disturbed ya," and the small man turned to walk away.

"No. It's fine, really," said Catherine, having fully recovered from her reverie, and now finding this man's appearance a respite from the aloneness she had felt for the last three days.

"I love to watch all the creatures, too. They're part of my world, ya know," said the man, and came and sat next to her on the picnic table. Catherine suddenly and inexplicably felt at ease — inexplicable because her experience of men had centred around one man to whom she had devoted herself, and while he never physically beat her, he had been her scourge of emotional and intellectual abuse.

"My name's Catherine," she said matter-of-factly.

"Well Kate, that's a good name, full of pure emotion, derives from the Greek, ya know. Nice to meet ya, and my name's Dion, but only for now, because as Gertrude Stein said, 'a rose is a rose is a rose,' meanin' of course that 'a rose by any other name would smell as sweet.'"

Catherine couldn't help but stare at the man. "Are you a writer?"

★

Back in her room, feeling somewhat refreshed, her thoughts were still upon her encounter on the beach. *How odd*, she thinks to herself, *he seems like an archtype, a simulacrum of some other being*. When she had asked if he was a writer, he seemed to riddle her with answers. For instance, "What good comes of a pen or keyboard?" he had queried, his eyes a-twinkle with mischievousness, and when she began to expound her literary aesthetics, he interrupted with, "But Kate, semen is silkier than ink." She could only look at him quizzically, yet knew he wasn't joking.

Finally when she was too stupefied to answer his verbal ripostes, he had laughed, "Well, in vino veritas," and had left her, his right hand waving like a flag in the wind, with a warm smile and a "Ta ta… see you again," his heavy boots crunching noisily in the sand.

Catherine looked at her laptop… *make sex a silhouette*, she reads to herself, as she reached for the bottle of Chianti on her desk to pour herself a glass. "In vino veritas", she salutes aloud as she takes a deep draught of the delicious ruby liquid, hoping she'd meet this Dion again.

★

The first memory you have is of lying in a crib. You know it's a crib because of the vertical slats surrounding you. A slanted light cuts through the darkness of the room. It comes from the open door, the door that is open to the room in which you rest. The illumination comes from the hallway beyond, and your eyes, not yet heavy with sleep, are drawn to the silhouette, a silhouette of a person, male or female unknown, since all detail is swallowed into darkness, a darkness that only eclipse creates.

You stare at the silhouette, the silhouette that is unmoving, but that you know is watching you, and you forget… and as you wake up, Catherine, you remember the dream, but have forgotten the consequences.

You lie in your bed, trying to remember if there were consequences, but to no avail — no other images are forthcoming. It is midnight, and you watch as a soft breeze billows the window curtains. Restless, you arise, don a light cotton blouse, shorts and sandals, deciding to take a night stroll, perhaps venture over to inspect that old lighthouse across the road from the Centre.

★

John Paul Rademuller, who had been a member of the Royal household staff of the Duke of Connaught in London, was its first keeper. He had emigrated to Upper Canada in the very early nineteenth century to start a school for German immigrants, but unfortunately the school had failed. Given his intelligence and stature, he was given the prestigious post of keeper of The Lake Light, the lighthouse built at Gibraltar Point in 1808.

As Catherine approached it, she remembered these details, as well as the fact that Rademuller had disappeared from his post in 1815, and it was suspected that he had been murdered, even though his body was never found. He had been known to be a brewer of bootleg beer that he sold to off-duty soldiers stationed at Fort York, and apparently, as rumour had it, he had refused to sell his brew to two drunken soldiers who thereupon slew him, dismembered his body and buried the parts around the island.

The Lake Light, as rumour had it, is haunted.

Standing before the structure under the illumination of a half moon, her first impression was of how small it was, being a mere eighty-two feet in height. The tower was hexagonal in shape, had small rectangular apertures vertically cut into its stone sides seemingly to act as windows, a small pagoda-like structure on its top that housed the lamp, and a single door for entrance and egress painted red and hinged with iron hardware in the shape of a sword. On this door, around waist level, Catherine noticed what seemed to be a rather large old-fashioned keyhole that piqued her curiosity. As she crouched and peered in with her right eye, she was instantly aware that the interior was lighted. She could see little detail except for what she presumed was the beginning of a spiral staircase.

Why would they keep a light on inside? Catherine asked herself. The lighthouse hadn't been used in decades, and was only preserved as an historic ornament. As she continued to peer through the keyhole, she slowly became aware that the usually consistent offshore island breeze had died, her ears simultaneously picking up a muffled sound as if something heavy were being dragged across a stone floor. Looking again through the keyhole, her eyes at first saw only what she had perceived before, but in a moment something moved across her field of vision. It went too quickly for her to catch any detail, but she was sure that it was a human form, bent over at the waist, and the upper torso clothed in some type of red jersey She stood up from her crouch and noticed that a fine low mist had encircled the base of the lighthouse, spreading out no more than twenty feet.

While she was not a superstitious person, and in fact was a confirmed atheist, her body wanted to move away and so she followed, quickly and quietly wending her way back to the Colony complex. As she went, she happened to glance back. It seemed that the lighthouse door was open, and the silhouette of a human figure stood in its frame. Whoever it was, she imagined, was watching her go.

★

She awoke next morning early from a fitful sleep, the memory of her visit to the lighthouse slowly emerging as she went about her ablutions and, while it had a phenomenological appeal, the night's experience was dismissed by her as a manifestation of an overactive imagination. The human figure she thought she saw was probably a convenient hallucination caused by the fear she had felt, and her glance back toward the lighthouse door had been extremely brief.

The day proved to turn gradually very hot and humid, and having had no success at her computer in writing anything, the sweat running down her back and brow while seated in her room which had no air-conditioning, she decided on a swim.

The beach on the lakeside of the island was a mere two-minute walk from the Centre. So having donned a modest bathing suit, grabbed a beach towel, a notebook and some cigarettes, she ventured forth and was soon ensconced upon the sand. For a while, she took inventory of her surroundings, watching the various forms of people and bird move through water or sky respectively. She simply looked and absorbed, not allowing her consciousness to fill with internal thoughts. Her eye wandered slowly and came to rest on the short figure that was plodding towards her. Something tingled in her as she watched her little simulacrum approach.

"My, Kate, what a fine figure you cut," said Dion as he drew up and stopped before her.

"A little short in the breast department, I'm afraid," replied Catherine who had no inhibitions about talking about human anatomy or sex.

"Well, I've always thought more than a handful is a waste," chuckled the little man, and asked, "May I join ya?"

"You may," she replied in a mock-regal manner, and gave a little laugh since she found his quaint and archaic verbal expressions lovely yet also humorous.

Dion plopped himself down on the sand in front of her.

"Do you believe in ghosts?" Catherine suddenly asked.

Dion's right eyebrow shot up, and he quizzed, "What sort of ghosts be they that you're askin' about?"

Catherine proceeded to relate her previous night's adventure at the lighthouse. As she spoke about the silhouetted figure in the lighthouse doorway, Dion's face took on a grim expression — his brow knitted, lips pursed and eyes in a fierce squint.

When Catherine finished speaking, Dion was quiet for a moment, then warned, "I'd be careful, Kate. I don't believe in ghosts, but if you saw what you saw, they also saw you, by the sounds of it. And if there's foul play going on, I wouldn't want to see you, an unfortunate bystander, become victim."

A cold feeling crept into Catherine as she looked into Dion's eyes. He suddenly smiled.

"But here I am scarin' ya, and you're probably right — just a figment. Come let's go for a short stroll down the beach, and you can tell me somethin' of your self. Must be some reason these unnatural imaginings are impressing upon you at this time."

Dion rose, took Catherine's hand and helped her stand. They walked down along the shore, and Catherine began talking of her past life.

★

That evening Catherine stepped out on to the back sun deck of the Centre, after having had a late supper, and lit a cigarette. She looked up at the stars in the dark sky which had the occasional cloud scudding by that was illuminated by the moon, while her mind nomadically moved through her memories of the day and her conversation with Dion. The little man had related some of his own background — his early childhood growing up on a remote Greek island, his studies at the University of Athens where he mastered in Oenology, his emigration to Canada and his subsequent pursuit of knowledge in the field of musical composition. Wine, women and song, he had said, were his fields of expertise. Catherine had laughed.

"But it's true," Dion had remonstrated in a satyrical way, "I can tell two wines apart, their grape and vineyard, by just their scent. The women all lust after me…"

Catherine laughed again.

"… and if music be the food of love," he said chuckling, and drew a small wooden flute from his right trouser pocket that he began to play, issuing forth a melody in pentatonics, a haunting melody with a long narrative arc before it repeated itself, conjuring visions in Catherine's mind of desolate windswept places.

Finishing her cigarette, she decided she'd walk over to the lighthouse and confirm her intimations that what she thought she had experienced was nothing more than a manufacture from her irrational neurosis.

When it came into view, her vision was instantly drawn to the bridge atop the lighthouse, for the lamp was a glowing beacon in the night. She stopped for an instant, wondering whether or not it was occupied, but then continued towards it, remembering that one of the artists at the Centre had told her the lamp was left on sometimes inadvertently by a Parks and Recreation guide who hosted school groups in tours.

She reached the lighthouse and, being curious, pulled at the metal ring that served as door handle. The door opened gently, but before she could look in, it burst open upon her with such force that she lost her balance and toppled to the ground.

"Such a pity. You should've minded your own business," said a gruff man's voice that issued from the silhouette in the lighthouse doorway.

Catherine attempted to get up, but the man was upon her in a flash, twining his left arm around her neck in a stranglehold. She tried to scream but couldn't and only ended up coughing as the man began violently dragging her towards the bushes some twenty feet from the lighthouse. Her head twisting, she saw the glint of metal in the man's free hand, and she began twisting and kicking but couldn't free herself, her mind now in full terror and discord.

Suddenly, borne through the night air, there erupted a thunderous roar like that of a giant untamed beast, and she heard an ominous tramping rush towards her. The arm around her neck was violently wrenched away, and when she looked up from the ground she saw her assailant dangling in the air, dangling on the end of a long muscular arm, the end of which was a huge hand that encircled her attacker's throat. As her eyes took in more, her mind tried to refuse her vision, but couldn't. Before her stood a humanoid creature at least seven feet in height. Its upper body showed a muscularly built man, it's head adorned with a wild mass of red hair and beard, but the lower body was not a man's. From the abdomen downwards, it was fully furred. Its legs displayed inversion where the knees would be, and they ended in large black, cloven hooves. It roared again, and Catherine's body shook. In one swoop motion, the creature swung the assailant's body and threw it with such force that when it hit the lighthouse wall it seemed to come apart.

Catherine's eyes widened as the man-thing approached, but was surprised when it gently helped her to her feet. Its left arm went about her waist and it drew her to him. She could smell its hot breath that seemed alcohol scented. But when she looked into those eyes, taking in the silver-coloured horizontal slit-shaped pupils set upon blood-shot white sclera, the shock deprived her of consciousness.

★

The Centre manager had told Catherine the next day that she had been found lying on the sun deck. A doctor had tended to her, having been present due to the commotion about the lighthouse. A tourist had spotted the mangled remains of her attacker when he had approached to take photographs of the building. The police upon inspection had found another body, crammed in the back of the lighthouse utility closet, that of a woman who had been stabbed, dismembered and stuffed in a large plastic garbage bag.

Catherine was questioned by a police inspector. She described an assault upon her, but lied, saying that she had passed out, and knew nothing of the demise of the mangled man. She was left for the rest of the day to recuperate, but the Centre manager watched over her and tended to her needs, for it was obvious that Catherine was suffering from severe shock. She sat in the sun in a dazed state until evening when she retired to her room.

The night came, and Catherine retired to her bed. Lying on her back and staring at the ceiling above, her mind was full of roiling clouds, clouds of images, memories of the day. Slowly a feeling of panic began to build in her as she could make no sense of her recent experiences. But then, through her open window, where a slight breeze moved her curtains, there came a sound — a flutey sound that began a slow and tender melody in pentatonics, a melody she had never heard before, a melody that calmed and warmed her soul, a melody that in its rhythm felt like a voice, a voice that spoke in a quaint and archaic manner.

RICHARD TRUHLAR

Richard Truhlar is the author of eight books of fictions and poetry: *Terminal Intelligence, The Hollow and other fictions, The Pitch, Dynamite in the Lung, Figures in Paper Time, Utensile Paradise, Parisian Novels*, and *A Porcelain Cup Placed There*, as well as a number of chapbooks, and numerous publications in national and international anthologies and periodicals. He is a fictioneer, poet, text/sound/music composer, visual artist, music producer, and editor/publisher. A founding member of the sound poetry group Owen Sound and the electroacoustic chamber music ensemble Tekst, he lives in Toronto. For more information, visit his web site at www.richardtruhlar.com

OTHER TITLES FROM TEKSTEDITIONS

A Cornucopia — Opal Louis Nations
A Few Sharp Sticks — Brian Dedora
Earth Becoming Sky — Guy Ewing
Way Down That Lonesome Road — Mark Miller
Mr. Body — Opal Louis Nations
The Port's Seasonal Rental — Gerry Shikatani
Permission To Speak: an anthology of new fiction
           — eds. Richard Truhlar & Beverley Daurio
Terminal Intelligence — Richard Truhlar

ALSO AVAILABLE FROM TEKSTEDITIONS
A Slice of Voice at the Edge of Hearing — Brian Dedora
The Battle of the Five Spot — David Lee